"Hello," she said, wearing a skimpy red negligee
meant to barely cover her, and doing a good job of it.
"Can I help you?"

"Yes, probably you can."

I could detect the lust in the air,
but that had nothing to do with the fact that I'm a good detective
and everything to do with the fact that I'm a man.
When it comes to emotional distress,
there's nothing like a mourning widow.
And let me tell you, Suzi Biggs was *nothing* like a mourning widow.
She was more like a morning window.
I could see right through her.

"I'm Benjamin Drake of the Always Reddy Detective Agency.
I'd like to speak with you about your husband's death."

"You mean murder!"

"Yeah, that's what I mean."

BY THE BALLS

The Persons this *Mystery* is about—

BENJAMIN DRAKE,
a detective with a passion for small cigars and Old Grand-Dad and a weakness
for women in trouble, is employed by the Always Reddy Detective Agency.

HAL REDDY,
a short, broad man with a wide nose and huge ears that stick out from his craggy,
bald head, is head of the Always Reddy Detective Agency.

RHODA CHANG,
quiet, mysterious, and full of information, is the Agency's receptionist and gal
Friday.

DINO,
the sanitation engineer at Penny's Lanes Bowling Center, is a mousy rail-thin guy
with investigative aspirations.

DUKE WELLINGTON,
a homicide detective in the Testacy City Police Department, is not fond of private
dicks in general and Ben Drake in particular. He has a loud mouth and loud
clothing.

MARK WEISNECKI,
a tall, mustachioed lunkhead of a detective, is Duke Wellington's partner.

ELIZABETH BIGGS,
spunky and far from frail, is Gentleman Joe's aged mother.

REBECCA HORTZBACH,
Testacy City's Medical Examiner, is a woman of academic beauty and a collector
of conspiracies and arcane facts. Known among the police as the crazy cat lady,
as much for her curiosity as for her appearance.

SUZI BIGGS,
Gentleman Joe's widow, is young, cute, and sexy. She seems to be dealing with
the death of her husband pretty well.

BY THE BALLS

●●

The Persons this *Mystery* is about—cont.

JERRY IVERSON,
a young, good-looking, up-and-coming bowler, is Gentleman Joe's protégé. Though he's a good bowler, he's even better with the ladies.

SPENCE NELSON,
the nattily dressed gentleman who rents shoes to eager bowlers at Penny's Lanes, is also a smooth-talking intellectual with a Ph.D. in genetics.

WALTER WILSON,
the diminutive owner of Van Winkle's Bar, is a retired world-class bowler. His right hand is missing its thumb and forefinger.

JACK WALKER,
curly-haired, clean-shaven, with a strong rock of a jaw, is the millionaire owner of Walker Industrial, Testacy City's top corporation. He smokes a pipe.

BUTCH and SCHULTZ,
Jack Walker's hulking Hindu bodyguards, are almost identical. They both know how to hit, and hit hard.

BRAD MAKOFF,
a short, ape-like little man, all forehead and belly with a wide, flat nose and thinning black hair, is one half of the most notorious vice partnership in Testacy City.

LEO NOLAN,
the other half of the notorious vice partnership, is tall and broad with ham-sized fists. His violent tendencies are legendary throughout the Testacy City underworld.

BOBBY REGARDIE,
a tall, lanky gent with a peculiar laugh, is the head animal keeper at the Wild Animal Reserve.

GENTLEMAN JOE BIGGS,
Testacy City's resident world-class bowler, is loved and admired by all of Testacy City. He also happens to be murder victim No. 1.

BY THE BALLS

● ●

What this *Mystery* is about—

● ● ● A family bowling center turns into a scene of BLOODY MURDER . . . An age-old CONSPIRACY is brought to light . . . A revealing visit to a LUXURIOUS BATHROOM . . . A promise of VIOLENCE at the hands of ANGRY BOWLERS . . . A hot CUP OF COFFEE becomes a reckless young man's only friend . . . A 20-foot orange extension cord becomes a DEADLY TOOL . . . An OVERLOOKED CLUE is found embedded in shag carpeting . . . A STRONG PAIR OF HANDS leave a mark where nobody was supposed to look . . . A botched set-up ends with a VIOLENT GUNFIGHT . . . A painful reminder from a LIPSTICK-STAINED cup . . . A single .38 BULLET provides a gleeful release for a demented man . . . An unlikely alliance reveals a WEB OF DECEIT.

Wouldn't You Like to Know—

- What would cause a bowling champ to get his head crushed between two bowling balls?
- Where to get the best chicken-fried steak in Testacy City?
- What an eight-letter word for "hairless" that starts with *g* is?
- How a much-maligned character can be clear and refreshing?
- What goes on in the bathroom at Penny's Lane Bowling Center?
- Why sleeping in the nude can be bad?
- What a sexy pathologist can tell you about the Illuminati, the U.S. government, and the Great Depression?
- What stirs the loins of a bowling groupie?

───────────

YOU will find the answers in this engaging tale of murder which is not only a brilliant mystery but also a fascinating excursion into the eclectic and absurd facets of life in a crime-filled desert city.

A BOWLING ALLEY MURDER MYSTERY

BY
THE
BALLS

By DASHIELL LOVELESS
a.k.a.
Tom Fassbender and Jim Pascoe

Authors' Dedication—
For GEORGE T. DELACORTE, JR. and LLOYD E. SMITH

Cover painting and all interior art by
PAUL POPE

UGLYTOWN PRODUCTIONS
Los Angeles, California
printed in the U.S.A.
DESIGNED AND PRODUCED BY TOM FASSBENDER AND JIM PASCOE

First Edition

Library of Congress Catalog Card Number: 98-86308

ISBN: 0-9663473-0-7

By the Balls Web address: http://www.uglytown.com/balls

Printed in the United States of America

10 9 8 7 6 5 4 3 2 1

BY THE BALLS

List of *Exciting* Chapters—

BY THE BALLS

List of *Thrilling* Illustrations—

BY THE BALLS

Chapter One

ANOTHER MISERABLE DAY IN TESTACY CITY

IT WAS A MISERABLE DAY in Testacy City. Rain clouds hung low over the flat expanse of the desert town, spewing forth torrents of water that turned the dirt-caked streets into rivers of mud. I've spent most of my life in either Testacy City, Las Vegas, or somewhere in between. Living in the desert has taught me to hate the rain. I prefer the dry air and near-constant sunshine that you normally find in the American Southwest. When it rains, trouble comes down.

The trouble started last night. I'd worked late, tracking down leads on a big jewel heist, and had come away with nothing but a name and a severe hangover. I thought I could handle my detective work better than that; hell, I thought I could handle my drinks better than that. A name, a hangover, and now I was late. And it was raining. It was a miserable day.

I climbed the steps to the offices of the Always Reddy Detective Agency, on the second floor of the William Kemmler Building at 1341 Fielding Avenue, right smack in the middle of Testacy City's business district. The newspaper I'd bought that morning, which had tried its best to shield me from the rain, was so much mush. I didn't own an umbrella; I don't think anyone in the city did. I tossed the news in the trash as I entered the office, nodding to Rhoda Chang, the Agency's gal Friday, and made my way down the hall to my corner. It was my little plot of workspace real estate, less than an office yet more than a cubicle. The place where I took calls and would hang up pictures of my wife and kids, if I had a wife and kids. I did have a wife once, but seeing her picture this morning wouldn't have helped my spirits any.

"Drake!" Hal Reddy's wrecking-ball-on-concrete voice smashed through the cluttered Agency offices, finding me just as I arrived at my desk.

"Yeah?" I shouted back.

"Get in here! Now!"

Normally, I didn't like to keep the boss waiting, but I needed to take a little detour through the Agency's small kitchen for a somewhat fresh cup of coffee. And with that small solace, I entered the smoky confines of Hal's office.

The boss sat behind his desk, chomping on a smoldering Antonio y Cleopatra, one of those dimestore cigars that come five to a box. He was a short, broad man with a wide nose and huge ears that stuck out at right angles from his craggy, bald head. The top half of his left ear was missing (a remnant of his days working homicide in Los Angeles back in the '60s), which made his right ear seem that much larger.

"Sit down, Drake."

He inhaled deeply from his cigar, and it sprang to life. Hal looked like a bear, and his squinty little eyes gave the impression of ignorance. But if you could hold his gaze— and few could—you'd see the cold fire of intelligence burning there.

"Know anything about bowling?" Hal asked, as he added to the volume of smoke that drifted about the office.

"Not much beyond the basics."

"The name Gentleman Joe Biggs mean anything to you?"

"No. I take it he was into bowling?"

"Not just *into* bowling; as far as Testacy City goes, he *was* bowling: PBA tour, endorsements, the whole bit."

"You said was…"

"That's right. Was. They found him dead at Penny's Lanes this morning. What's the matter with you? Don't you read the papers?" Hal punctuated this point with a deep draw on his cigar.

"Christ, give me a break! I just got in."

"Then you should get in earlier." He pointed at me with the glowing tip of his stogie.

"Come on, Hal. You didn't call me in here to bawl me out for being late. What gives?"

He took one of the many manila envelopes that littered his desk and pushed it toward me.

"I'm giving you the Biggs case."

"What? But I'm working on the Haufschmidt jewel heist." Looked like last night was a total bust.

"Yeah, I know that. Tell me how far along you are."

I winced at the thought of letting Hal down; I didn't have nearly enough to justify him keeping me on the case. I was half-tempted to lie but knew that wouldn't play with the boss. Hal was the best detective I knew. He had plenty of experience with lies—both telling them and seeing through them.

"Just got started. I did a little digging yesterday and came up with Marcel the Mangler."

"Isn't he that French jewel thief who got sent up after he strangled a street mime?"

"That's the one. The word on the street says he's in town, recently out of Leavenworth."

"You got any leads on this French fry?"

"Nope. It took me all night just to shake his name loose."

"That's what happens when you read the morning paper in the afternoon: you lose the jump shot," Hal chided. He leaned back in his chair. "I gave that case to Henry Goiler this morning."

"Goiler?"

I had nothing against Goiler, even though he was a slob and a braggart. He'd worked a couple of jobs with me, and I found him to be handy on a caper. It just rankled me that I was being replaced on a case.

"Yeah, he's already got something on Marcel," Hal explained. "Apparently they did the cat and mouse a couple of years ago."

I couldn't really argue with that, plus the truth of the matter was I didn't really like the case. I didn't have a whole lot, and I'd had a rotten time getting what little I did have.

"Fair enough," I relented. "So now I've got the bowling alley butcherer. What do we know?"

I flipped open the file. Except for the facts that Joe Biggs was 5'10", 207 pounds, 54 years old, and dead, it was nearly empty.

"That's about it," Hal said, indicating the folder. "Biggs was found about nine this morning by the guy who cleans the place. His head was in the ball return on lane 13, smashed between two bowling balls."

"So who's our client?"

"The mother, Elizabeth Biggs. She lives at the Desert Flower Retirement Complex. Apparently the cops gave her the impression that they were more interested in running Joe's name through the mud than finding his killer."

"Any other family?"

"I hear he's got a wife. Don't know much about her. No kids. He's got a house in Victory Gardens."

Victory Gardens was the high-class suburb of Testacy City. If you lived there you were money—old or new, it didn't matter.

"So he was doing all right, huh?"

"Guess so," Hal shrugged. "Get out and interview the mother. See what she's got. Then talk to the widow."

"I'm on it."

I grabbed the sparse Biggs file and left Hal to his smoke. There's something about a new case that really gets the blood pumping. I grabbed my hat and hit the road, blowing Rhoda a kiss on the way out.

Chapter Two

THE CRIME SCENE

A FEW MINUTES LATER I was navigating Testacy City's barren streets in my powder-blue '65 Galaxie 500, heading toward Penny's Lanes. I didn't necessarily agree with Hal's plan of visiting the mother first. I thought my time would be better spent at the crime scene, especially since the body was discovered only a few hours ago. I was pretty sure the mother wasn't going anywhere fast, but I couldn't say the same thing about any evidence still at the scene of the crime.

I took a left off Broadway onto Dickerson and drove past the bowling alley, slow enough to take in the details but fast enough not to raise suspicion. Just another rubbernecker. The place was crazy with cops; there were six black-and-whites parked out front and four uniforms managing the barricade.

I parked my car in the next block. The rain had slowed to a misty drizzle. It still didn't make me happy, but at least I could walk a block without getting soaked. I pulled my hat low on my forehead and got to walking.

It's no secret that cops and private eyes don't always get along. But this morning I didn't see any unmarked cars in front of the alley or in the parking lot of the diner next door. Without any detectives around, the direct approach might work best.

My gut feeling paid off. John McCluskey, a friend of mine in the Testacy City Police Department, was on duty outside the barricade. We go way back to my days as a fireman; his wife was a high school friend of mine.

He saw me coming. "Hey, Drake! How are ya?"

He stuck out his hand. I shook it.

"Good, thanks," I lied. "How about you?"

"You know me, I'm a tiger," he countered. He pointed toward the bowling alley with his solid chin. "Hell of a thing for a Monday morning, huh?"

"Yeah. You got the skinny?"

"Well, first I gotta warn ya. Duke Wellington told us that that no one but officers and witnesses go in."

Homicide detective Duke Wellington wasn't fond of private dicks in general and me in particular. A couple of years back I took a case he'd solved and solved it right. He hasn't forgotten about it.

"He mention me by name?" I asked.

"No, but it's no secret you're included."

"That was expected, I guess. Can you at least fill me in on what went down here?"

His head swiveled on his beefy neck, first left, then right as he glanced over his shoulders, confirming that no one was close enough to hear us talk. "You didn't hear it from me," he cautioned.

"Not a problem." I meant it.

"Okay then. The janitor, a guy named Dino, found the body about nine. It's been here since early this morning, probably about two or three. They just took it out about fifteen minutes ago."

"What was this guy doing here at three in the morning?"

I know the answer was obvious. It was just hard for me to conceive of anyone wanting to bowl at that time of the night.

"According to Dino, this guy liked to bowl from one a.m.—when the place closes—until about three. I guess it was easier for him to concentrate on his game."

"Right," I chuckled. "I don't suppose you can look the other way for a second or two..."

He slowly shook his head no. "This place has a set of rear doors," he continued. "We think the killers used them to get in and out quick and quiet."

I took the hint. "Thanks, John. See ya around."

"Sure thing, Drake. You too."

I ambled away and headed across the diner's parking lot, making my way toward the back of the alley. A couple of cops were milling around, but there were also enough parked cars to make it look like I had business being there.

I got to the back of the building and tried the double doors. Locked. Damn. As I moved away to contemplate my next move, I heard the distinctive cla-clack of a steel door opening. Out walked a mousy little guy in his late 40s. He was rail thin, dressed in a denim shirt and pants, lugging a huge bag of trash. He looked like a convict. I shook the dice and took a guess that this was my man.

"Yo, Dino!" I rolled.

He turned around, jumping a couple of feet in the air. It's always good to be right. He shifted himself into a stance that suggested he might know how to deal a little damage. I was too pressed for time to try him out.

"'Morning. I'm Ben Drake." I extended my hand. It was that kind of day.

He took my hand and pumped it, relief etched on his face. He seemed a little skittish.

"So whatcha want?"

"I'm a private detective." I handed him a card.

He turned it over in his hands before shoving it into his back pocket. "A P.I., huh?"

"Yeah, the genuine article."

"Mebbe I can help ya."

"That's what I'm hoping," I encouraged. There's a part of everyone that wants to be a detective.

"Let's go inside where it's dry," he suggested after thinking things over. That was just the invitation I was waiting for.

He led me into the eerie, industrial atmosphere of the back room. Ahead of us, down a short set of steps, row upon row of identical robots with gaping maws of steel lay silent and motionless. A narrow catwalk built atop the machines and an equally narrow walkway—little more than a crawlspace—between the back wall and the machines were the only paths available to get from one side to the other. I could only imagine the noise and madness that filled the air back here when the alley was in full swing.

"Take a right here," Dino instructed, just as I was about to enter the guts of the alley.

Instead we walked past a long workbench littered with a wide variety of tools and went through another door into the part of the bowling alley that most people see. We weren't alone; a handful of forensics types and a few blues were hanging about. I tried to act inconspicuous, but a guy in a fedora and a rumpled suit is bound to attract attention sooner or later. Especially in a bowling alley.

"Mebbe I can shadow someone for ya, like in the movies?"

"Maybe," I was feeling rushed. "Tell you what I need right now, though—"

"Yeah? So I can help?" Dino interrupted.

"Yeah," I talked fast, suspecting I wouldn't have much longer. "Here's what I need you to do. In my experience, cops got a lot to do and sometimes they get sloppy. It's almost a guarantee they miss something at the crime scene. So if you see something suspicious, give me a call."

Dino looked a little disappointed. "So—"

"Aw, sweet Jesus, Mary, and Joseph, don't tell me that's Ben Drake!" a booming voice bounced off the walls, cutting Dino off. "Someone gimme a stick so as I can beat the man who let this rapscallion onto my crime scene!"

Duke Wellington found me. He was heading right at me, eyes filled with hatred. He wore a wine-colored suit with a bright green neon tie; he looked more like a pimp than a homicide detective.

He closed the thirty-foot gap between us with a few strides of his long legs. "You got no business being in this building!" He shoved a huge finger in my face. It was attached to a huge fist; a fist I'd felt once before and was not anxious to feel again.

"Easy, man. I'm just working a case, like you."

"You're working this case? You're working this case?" He was the type who liked to hear himself talk. "Now who in high holy Heaven hired you?"

"You know I can't tell you that, DW. Client confidentiality and all."

Duke Wellington's dark skin began to blossom red. The muscles of his jaw jumped out from his face as he clenched his teeth. I could tell he wanted to hit me. He turned toward Dino instead.

"You don't be talkin' to this guy," he gestured in my direction with a wild waving of his arms. "You find anything, you talk to me, Duke Wellington! Got it?"

"Yeah, but…" Dino tried to explain.

"But nothin'! I'm the guy you talk to, understand? I am the guy."

"Yeah, yeah. No problem," Dino caved.

"Good," Duke Wellington purred before his attention swung back my way. "You get outta here."

"Come on. I've gotta earn my paycheck," I pleaded. I didn't think it would get me too far.

"O'Neal!" Duke Wellington shouted toward one of the uniformed cops. "This guy seems to be lost. Help him find the way out."

A brawny cop with a cruel mouth headed toward me, drawing his baton and gesturing my way. "Let's go, buddy," he ordered.

I shrugged at Dino and began the trek toward the front door. O'Neal marched behind me, prodding me with his stick.

On the way out I heard Duke Wellington giving Dino the third degree. Duke Wellington was a good detective; he had a keen sense of deductive reasoning. But that's only one thing a detective needs. What he lacked was people skills. You can do all the deductive reasoning you want, but it'll get you nothing if people won't talk to you. I didn't mind that Duke Wellington had kicked me off the scene; I got what I came for. I had a man on the inside.

"Now beat it, tough guy," O'Neal commanded when we reached the front door.

I walked the block back to my car, stopping at the diner for a cup of coffee to go. It was just about noon, and I was feeling good about my progress, especially after the dead end I'd hit last night.

I hadn't had a cigar all morning, so I pulled out a tin of J. Cortès Grand Luxes, the small dry-cured numbers I like to smoke. These aren't big stogies like Hal is fond of. They're much smaller, close to the size of cigarettes. I never seem to have enough time to finish off a nice Churchill, so these do the trick.

I fired up a smoke, then I fired up my car and headed out to see my client, Elizabeth Biggs.

Chapter Three

THE GRIEVING MOTHER

THE DESERT FLOWER RETIREMENT COMPLEX was a pensioner's community a stone's throw north of the city. I wasn't really looking forward to this interview. I didn't expect Elizabeth Biggs to be able to tell me much about her son's death, and it's never any fun dealing with relatives of the recently dead.

The sparse traffic on the road made my drive go quickly, and before long I pulled into the barren gravel lot and parked my car. It didn't look like this place got too many visitors. I opened my car door, then paused and sat for a moment, pulling out my cigars. I contemplated smoking one but decided against it, realizing I was stalling. I began a slow walk to the gated entrance, the gravel of the lot crunching under my shoes.

I went through a door underneath a small tin sign that told me it was the office. I was alone. On the right a couple of lonely padded benches rested below a paint-by-numbers flower picture. Straight ahead a short hallway opened into a large room filled with ill-arranged furniture and a single, small television against the far wall. To my left, the office proper reminded me of a dentist's waiting room. Above the narrow counter was a pair of sliding glass windows, beyond which was a small room with desk and chair. But no receptionist.

I waited a moment, the silence antiseptic around me. Losing patience, I slapped the metal bell that sat on the ledge. Its tinny sound seemed too loud in the emptiness.

Sooner than I thought, but not as soon as I would have liked, the door on the opposite side of the small office opened and a plump woman wearing a grey nurse's outfit and too much hairspray stumbled in. She looked annoyed.

"Yes?" She glared at me as she smoothed the wrinkles in her skirt.

"I'm Ben Drake, a private detective." I pressed my card to the glass. "I'm looking for Elizabeth Biggs."

"Oh, this must be about her son?" It was a statement, but she turned it into a question.

"Yes, that's right. Where can I find her?"

She bent over the desk and consulted a long list of names that lived under the clear blotter. "Uhhh, she's in D-109." More smoothing.

I waited to see if she'd give me directions. It seemed that was too much to ask. I started to doubt this woman's ability to help the elderly. "And where can I find that?"

"Go out the door there," she said, indicating the door I came in. "Take a right, and it's the third building on your left."

"Thanks."

I turned to leave.

She stopped me.

"By the way, there's no smoking in the Desert Flower Retirement Complex, sir."

"I'm not smoking."

She flashed me a smile that wasn't a smile.

"Just for your information."

I flashed back.

"Right. Thanks."

I turned again. This time I got out.

I followed my friend's directions and took a right down the path. I knew I was going to have a little trouble. The crooked trail ran around and between the eight buildings that randomly littered the courtyard. I couldn't tell which building was the third on my left, and I sure wasn't going back to ask for directions again, so I forged ahead.

The courtyard was a regular Garden of Eden. A variety of well-tended plants and trees grew along the curving path, filling the air with a not unpleasant fragrance. Some would have called it serene. Others would have described it as pastoral. To me, it was just a confounding maze. Occasionally, I bumped into an elderly Adam or Eve, wandering about as if they were on a mission to wander.

I'd been wandering for a while myself, when I noticed a big "F" on the building in front of me. I turned around, retraced my steps, and it wasn't long before I was pushing the button labeled "109" at the front door of the "D" building. An old woman's voice crackled through the small speaker.

"Who is it?"

"It's Ben Drake, ma'am. I'm from the Always Reddy Detective Agency."

"Oh, I'm glad you found me. Hold on a moment." I waited until the buzzer sounded to let me in.

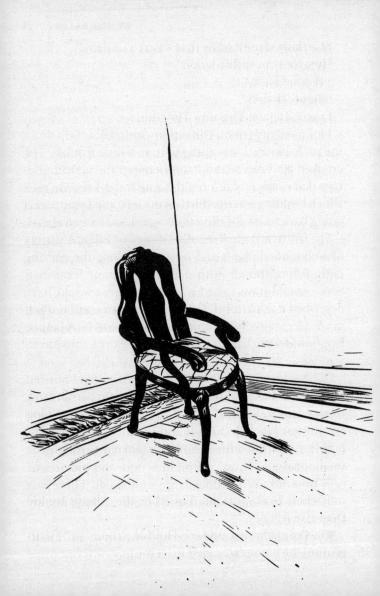

Her room was easier to find. I knocked on the door.

"Who is it?"

"It's still Ben Drake, ma'am."

"Oh, come in."

I grasped the doorknob. It resisted my attempt to turn it. "Ah, could you unlock the door, please?"

A moment passed before the door opened. "I'm sorry, this horrible business has me in a state."

Elizabeth Biggs was a small, white-haired woman, but she was far from frail. She wore a navy cardigan over a conservative white blouse and tan slacks. On her feet were a pair of white orthopedic shoes, the type nurses wear. Although her smile beamed brightly under her sapphire blue eyes, it didn't hide the pain.

"No problem, ma'am. Can I come in?"

"Oh, yes. I'm sorry. I've forgotten my manners. I just put on a new pot of coffee," she gestured toward the kitchen. "Could I offer you a cup?"

Apparently she hadn't forgotten them for long. I accepted.

She switched off the television and told me to take a seat on the sofa, which filled most of the small living room. The opposite wall was nothing short of a shrine to Gentleman Joe, with numerous portraits of him at various ages, pictures of him in action, and pictures of him brandishing trophies large and small. There was something missing, though, and I couldn't quite put my finger on it.

My thoughts were interrupted when Elizabeth brought in a tray holding two steaming cups of coffee along with a pitcher of cream and bowl of sugar. She placed her burden, appropriately, on the coffee table and sat down next to me.

"Now what did you want to ask me, Mr. Drake?"

I selected my cup and began with the basics. "I know the police came by earlier—"

"Those hooligans!"

Judging from that, I guessed it was Duke Wellington who had paid her the visit. "Yeah, the police don't know how to treat a lady. What'd they say to you?"

"Only the most terse and uncouth comments about Joey."

"Such as?"

"They wanted me to believe he was into bad things like gambling ..." she paused and made a face as if she had just eaten something disagreeable, "and drugs."

"We know that isn't true." I did my best to sound matter-of-fact.

"Absolutely not. He was a perfect gentleman. I raised him myself, you know. Ever since my husband Barry passed away. He's the one who taught my Joey to bowl."

"Did Joe have a lot of friends?" Somehow I couldn't bring myself to call him Joey.

"Friends? Sure. Everybody was Joey's friend..."

I sensed she wasn't quite finished talking, so I took a sip from my cup. It was a pause I regretted; she started to cry. It made me feel like leaving, but I knew I had to stay.

I got up and grabbed a couple of tissues from the box on the end table. As she took them, she struggled to compose herself.

"Thank you. He really was a good man. He was all I had."

"Did you see him often?"

"All the time. He came by and spent some time with me every day."

"So you were close, then?"

"Oh yes. I raised him, you know. Barry, Joey's father, died when Joey was only ten. That's how he got into bowling."

"You said that Barry taught Joe how to bowl."

"That's right. But Barry, God rest his soul, was not that good. Not that he was bad, he just wasn't good enough to bowl professionally. After he died, Joey practiced real hard every day. He was a natural, they said. He got on the pro circuit when he was 19—the youngest bowler ever on the tour. And he won. I was so proud of him. And I know Barry was too."

As interesting as this was, I had to get to the heart of the matter. I needed to know if Joe had any enemies. I started to transition with the old standard: "I know this is a hard time for you and his widow…"

Without warning the soft warmth of Elizabeth's face grew hard and cold; looked like that was the wrong thing to say. Then it hit me what was bothering me about the Joe Biggs photo gallery: no pictures of him with his wife—or any woman for that matter. Maybe it was the right thing to say after all.

"Ooooh! I don't like her," Elizabeth's voice was filled with hatred. "She's such a spiteful woman. I've known plenty of women like her before, always looking for something for nothing. And she's the type who always gets what she wants." She was really getting steamed over the younger Mrs. Biggs.

"I used to live with Joey—until he married that fast-moving hussy," she continued. "They got married two years ago, and she moved in with us. She didn't like having me around, so she told Joey it was either me or her, and Joey stuck me here. Not that I blame him. He was in love. We do such stupid things for love."

I told her I couldn't argue with her.

"You talk to that girl, Mr. Drake."

It wasn't a request.

"If I were a gambling woman, I'd bet good money she had something to do with Joey's death."

"I plan to do that later today, Mrs. Biggs," I assured her. "Look, I'd best be going, I have a few things to do before I talk to her."

"Oh, won't you stay just a little longer?" she pleaded. "There's more coffee…"

I glanced at my watch. I did have a little time to kill. And the coffee was good. Damn good. "All right. I'll have another cup."

She smiled, delighted, and took the cup from me as she hurried into the kitchen. Any trace of her anger over Suzi Biggs had disappeared with my decision to stay. And I found myself feeling good about that.

"Let me show you some pictures, Benny," she invited when she returned with my coffee. Only two people called me Benny, my grandmother and my wife. Both were dead. It was hard to take, but if I was going to let anyone call me Benny, it would be Elizabeth Biggs.

After showing me all the framed photos of Joe, she started in on the photo albums. We were halfway through the second album before I'd finished the pot of coffee, and it was time for me to go. It was still a fight to get out the door, and I felt a small pang of guilt about leaving.

I wound my way back through the courtyard, lighting a cigar as I got to my car. Then I headed back into town. Like I'd told Elizabeth, I had a few errands to run before I took on the widow Biggs.

Chapter Four

IN THE CUTTING ROOM

EVENTUALLY MY ERRANDS took me to the county morgue, a facility that smelled like stale cigarettes and dead bodies. Laid out in front of me on an aluminum autopsy table was the lifeless body of Gentleman Joe Biggs. His broad chest was neatly stitched with the traditional post-autopsy "Y." His head was deformed, with a strange, oblong appearance and eyes that popped out, giving him a permanent expression of cartoon-like, eternal surprise.

My tour guide was Testacy City's Medical Examiner, Rebecca Hortzbach, a woman of academic beauty, the type of girl you find attractive but are afraid to approach. A bob of red hair framed her pale, lightly freckled face. Over her bright green eyes she wore pointed glasses that accentuated her already feline appearance. A lit cigarette was almost always dangling from her mouth—even when she talked. Today was no exception.

"The proximate and immediate cause of death was extreme trauma to the head," she explained, indicating Biggs' misshapen skull. "And I mean *extreme* trauma to the head."

Rebecca wiped her hands on her white lab coat and sucked in a lungful of smoke. "In layman's terms, his head was crushed between two bowling balls. I'd say 16 pounders."

She had an uncanny eye for detail. She had solved more cases for the TCPD by simply looking at the crime scene than they'd care to admit. The police often referred to her as the crazy cat lady, as much for her curiosity as for her appearance. It was not meant as a compliment. Although I didn't care for the nickname, I had to admit she was a little freaky. There's something about a cute gal who likes cutting up dead bodies that gives me the willies.

She was also a collector of conspiracies and arcane facts. Every time I visited, she launched into some crazy theory of hers. My last time here she told me the story of how, in 1933, the U.S. government made a secret deal with the Illuminati to bring the country out of the Depression. In exchange for their aid, the Illuminati demanded their thirteen-story pyramid appear on the reverse of the new dollar bills. She went on to say that this pyramid represents the impending destruction of the Church and the establishment of a one-world government in its place.

"Any questions?" she asked.

By the look of his corpse, Biggs kept himself in pretty good shape. It would have been quite a task to wrestle him down and stave in his head with a pair of bowling balls. It made me wonder: "Was he drugged?"

"Toxicology shows no drugs or alcohol in his system. The guy was in excellent health. Hell, when I cut him open, his lungs were bright pink." The cigarette between her lips bobbed and danced as she spoke. "You normally only see that on kids."

"So, he just lay there while they cracked his head open?" I asked, hoping for her take on the murder. I got it.

"Probably not. Here's how it went down. This contusion," she lifted what remained of Biggs' head and pointed at a black-and-blue spot at the base of his skull, "is the result of him getting whacked from behind by a blackjack. My guess is that someone kept his attention while a second guy came up from behind and brained him.

"Then while he was down, they bound his hands behind his back and propped him in the ball return. Look here," she indicated Biggs' wrists. "You can see ligature marks from where he was tied. I found fibers of common household twine embedded there."

"Seems like a lot of trouble to go through to rub a guy out," I offered.

"Maybe not," she postulated. "My guess is that he knew something our perps needed to know, otherwise why tie him up? When he came to, they grilled him again. He still wouldn't cave, so smash!" She slammed her hands together. "They caved him."

I nodded. It was a good hypothesis. I had the how, now I just had to find the who and the why.

"Do you want to see the crime scene photos?" she invited.

"Sure."

Although I didn't expect them to show me anything I didn't already know, I followed her into her office. She handed me a folder that contained numerous black-and-white snapshots of Gentleman Joe at the crime scene taken from a variety of angles. It was a grisly sight. Biggs' head lay in the ball return, a single black bowling ball on either side. His body was stretched out, arms tied behind him, with something—I guessed a small stool—supporting his back. Blood was spattered everywhere. The ball return track and the top third of Biggs' bowling shirt were dark with blood. His pants were undone, revealing a pair of boxers, complete with cartoon bowling pins emblazoned upon them. For some reason, this disturbed me more than the manner of his death.

"Why are his pants undone?"

"That happens with a lot of dead bodies." She finished her cigarette and ground its remains into an overflowing ashtray. "Mainly men."

"No kidding. Why would that be?" I asked, a mix of dread and anticipation in my voice.

"I don't know for sure, but here's my theory," she said as she lit another cigarette. "It's a red herring. There's this long-standing tradition among more accomplished criminals to throw off medical examiners by introducing a bit of absurdity to the crime."

"Come on," I doubted as I joined her in a smoke. I had to get the smell of death out of my nostrils. "You can't expect me to believe that."

"Believe what you want," she dismissed with a wave of her hand, "but it's true. This goes back to the 1800s when forensic science was not so exact, and it was easier to throw a pathologist off the right track."

She looked at her watch. "Say Drake, you wanna grab some dinner? I haven't eaten all day."

I liked Rebecca. A lot. She was funny, intelligent, attractive—everything a guy like me looks for in a girl. If I were looking.

"I'll take a rain check," I responded truthfully, holding out for a meal that didn't happen right after I'd seen a dead body. "I've got to see the mourning widow before it gets too late."

"Next time, then." A smile of disappointment.

"Next time," I promised. I sent her a smile of encouragement, tipped my hat and left, footsteps echoing hollowly off the walls.

I exited into the chill evening air, feeling a little depressed. I'd never be caught dead in cartoon boxer shorts.

Chapter Five

THE MOURNING WIDOW

VICTORY GARDENS IS ALL MONEY. Looking around at the houses, you'll see either modern opulence punctuated with an occasional Victorian quaintness or monuments to old money updated here and there with the best of contemporary detail. It all boils down to how you were raised and what you're expecting. Me, I was expecting a bowler's house and a bowler's widow. When I navigated the car past the carved stone entranceway of Victory Gardens, I knew I was in for some surprises.

I pulled up to 300 Pine Lane and exhaled the last breath of smoke from my tiny cured cigar. The smoke formed lingering swirls in my car as I turned off the ignition and rolled up the window. Something made me want to stay there one moment longer. I sat looking at the facade of the Biggs' residence until I instinctively grabbed for another smoke, then I knew my moment was over. So I brushed off my lapels, got out of the car, and headed up the walkway to meet Mrs. Biggs.

Next to its neighbors, the Biggs house looked small and old—someone interested in houses might say cozy, though I was sticking to small and old. If I were forced to be poetic, I'd have said it was like a gingerbread house. But, thankfully, no one was forcing me.

I cringed a bit when I saw the beware-of-dogs sign,

dogs being the scourge of mailman and detective alike. And even though the rain had stopped, it was still plenty wet. Just thinking of wet dogs made me cringe again.

At the front door I pushed a small pearl-colored button I took to be the doorbell. A low, two-tone gong sounded, as if even the doorbell were grieving.

I heard the yipping of dogs: small dogs, the kind you can kick if they get in your way. When I had begun debating whether to endure the doorbell again or simply pound on the door, the locks clicked and the door opened. And there stood Mrs. Suzi Biggs.

"Hello," she said, wearing a skimpy red negligee meant to barely cover her, and doing a good job of it. "Can I help you?"

"Yes, probably you can."

I could detect the lust in the air, but that had nothing to do with the fact that I'm a good detective and everything to do with the fact that I'm a man. When it comes to emotional distress, there's nothing like a mourning widow. And let me tell you, Suzi Biggs was *nothing* like a mourning widow. She was more like a morning window. I could see right through her.

"I'm Benjamin Drake of the Always Reddy Detective Agency. I'd like to speak with you about your husband's death."

"You mean murder!"

"Yeah, that's what I mean."

"Well, come on in. Don't mind the dogs. They're friendly." Then, more for my benefit than for the dogs, she commanded, "Laza! Apsos! Settle down, you two!

This man's here to help us." Back to me. "You *are* here to help, right?"

"Sure."

I set my hat on a tiny table near the door, then she led me into the main living room, the damn dogs nipping at my heels. We sat down in a pair of matching red leather arm chairs. I tried to stay focused despite the number of trinkets, trophies, and other bowling knickknacks scattered about the room—and despite her skimpy red negligee.

Before I could start my questions, she came at me with: "So, *how* can I help you, Ben—that's your name, right?"

"What do you know about murder, Mrs. Biggs?"

"Only what I read in the novels," she giggled and turned coyly away with a hand to her smile. I didn't know if she was trying to be cute or if she was tipsy. I knew she'd been drinking; I could smell the faint tang of alcohol in the room.

"By the way, you can call me Suzi." She stopped talking and looked around the big colonial-style living room, her smile fading into melancholy. I caught her gaze stop on a portrait of Joe over the fireplace. Her mood changed quickly and melodramatically. ". . . And of course I know my husband was murdered."

"Of course. Know anybody who'd want him that way?"

"If you're asking me if I know who killed him, the answer, Ben, is no. This wouldn't be a detective story if I knew who the killer was."

I hadn't wanted the questions to start out this antagonistic, but since we were already warming up with the verbal fisticuffs, I tried this combo: "Funny, when I talked with his mother, she said you …"

Suzi exploded. "Don't even tell me she said I did it!" She was on her feet, her pink-nailed fingers rubbing her temples. "That bitch!"

"Hold on, young lady. Don't get all excited and start jumping to conclusions. Now, it's no secret how you gals feel about each other. Why don't you give me the Suzi Biggs side of the story."

"I'm sorry for acting like that. Ben, she makes me crazy. And it's her who doesn't like me; I don't have a problem with her other than that." She was already heading for the liquor cabinet when she turned this trick, "If you want us to have a real discussion, you're gonna have to drink with me."

"Not going to argue with that."

"What do you want?"

"Old Grand-Dad, if you've got it."

She threw me a look that said try again. Before I could, she asked, "Is that some kind of brandy?" How did I forget she was twenty-four?

"Ah, it's bourbon. Do you have any bourbon?"

Her laughter kept me company while she worked the drinks. She brought over a goddamn water glass full of hooch. Looked like she was going to shoot tequila. Brave. And it could play to my advantage.

"So, why doesn't the old lady like you?" I started in again.

"You must not be that good of a detective if you can't figure that one out. I'm … what some people would say … 'significantly younger' than Joe. Mama Biggs couldn't understand our love. She thought it was all about his money."

"But it was really true love?"

She downed her second shot, still managing to pause long enough to make me suspect her reply.

"Well, yeah. When I met Joe, I never thought I'd fall for a bowler. But he really was a gentleman. He really paid attention to me, treated me like I was some kind of important person." Her eyes were drifting off. She was getting full of drama again.

"I believe you, Suzi." I lied. "Just one more question."

I took a long pull off the bourbon, giving her time to have more of the Mexican poison. She seemed to enjoy my attempt at conversational tension.

"Can you think of anyone else, besides Joe's mother, who may have been unhappy about your marriage? An old flame, maybe?"

"Nobody." She hung on that word as she licked the lime juice off the tips of her fingers, seemingly lost in thought.

Liquor makes people either talkative or unreasonably quiet. It was clear what camp we were in. I wasn't going to get any answers, and until I had more of an angle, I didn't really have any more questions. I took my last swallow of bourbon, set the glass down, and said, "Well, Suzi, I just have one favor to ask: may I use your bathroom?"

She escorted me to the first-floor bathroom. True enough, I had to use it; but over the years, I'd found that you could learn a lot about a person by using their john.

Here was the layout: deep-basin sink, round mirror above, standard head, no shower, hardwood floor, mauve throw rugs, matching mauve hand towel, lots of plants. The thing that most caught my attention was a framed photo of Gentleman Joe wearing nothing but a Speedo. He was striking a weight lifter's pose in the midst of an array of fallen bowling pins. Cute.

Before I flushed, I figured I'd try something. With one hand on the door to steady it, I slowly, silently turned the knob with the other. When I got the door open, I could hear Suzi's voice. Stretching my neck to catch a glimpse of the scene, I saw her motioning to someone I couldn't see. Her hushed voice seemed to be telling this mysterious third party to stay put.

Now that I had a clue, I slipped the door back into place, flushed, then audibly opened the door. When I reentered the room, Suzi looked as if nothing were going on; in fact, too much so.

"Are you done with me, Ben?"

Her smile was playful, almost enticing; paradoxically her body language exhibited the most modesty I'd seen since my arrival. She stood legs crossed, elbows pinned inward, trying in vain to cover herself, or at least giving the illusion of caring to. This girl knew her game.

"I'm done asking you questions, for now." I turned to the door and retrieved my hat. Then giving her the game right back, I said, "You know, it's not a good idea being alone at a time like this. Maybe you should call somebody, like a mother or a sister."

"Why, Ben, that's awful sweet of you to think about my

needs like that. Oh, but my Mama's dead, and I'm an only child. I'll be all right. I . . . I can call you if I have any problems?"

"Of course you can. I hope you do . . . if you have any problems, I mean." I handed her my card, and then I was out.

The bourbon made me want to smoke, but for whatever reason I didn't feel like burning the tobacco in the Biggs house. I've got a deep-down respect for the fairer sex. Sure, she wasn't playing straight with me. But in this business it doesn't take long to realize that nobody tells the truth, at least not all the time.

I would have plenty of opportunity to smoke in the car, because my next move was crystal clear. It was Suzi who made a passing joke about this being a detective story, and as it goes in all good detective stories, it was now time to stake out the widow's house to see what might develop. Especially considering she most definitely had a mysterious visitor.

My small cigar had not even reached its end when out from Suzi's door came yet another clue: a young chap, tall, clean-cut, and good-looking. He was wearing a checkered button-down shirt opened in front with a white T-shirt underneath. What most caught my attention were the nice pair of black-and-white saddle shoes. You can't tell whether to trust somebody based only on his shoes—and this was one fella I wasn't trusting—still, you gotta like a guy with a fancy set of soles.

He kept twisting his head left and right, looking like he

was trying to spot someone—probably me. I'd have to be extra careful shadowing him. If I could let him get out of Victory Gardens without his putting the make on my tail, I'd have him.

When we were both on the open road, I knew I was out of his mind. One of the Ben Drake rules of shadowing is not to be focused on your target too much; it's too easy to show your hand. I eased back just enough and looked up over the road. The Testacy City sun set low in the sky. It made the sand swirling off the plains glow red like neon dust.

The moment we hit the city, I had that strange feeling of knowing where we were headed. I'd be damned if we weren't right back at the bowling alley. Good ol' Penny's Lanes.

Chapter Six

JERRY GOES BOWLING

WHEN I ENTERED THE BOWLING ALLEY, the low rumble of rolling balls and the crash of falling pins immediately overwhelmed me. Some twangy country-western music played in the background. Lane thirteen, with its lights off, was noticeably vacant. Maudlin bowlers had piled dozens of colorful bouquets at the foul line. I guess everyone did love Gentleman Joe.

Our man went over to a locker and pulled out his own ball and shoes. I was still new to this bowling stuff, but my keen detective skills were telling me that this guy was a serious bowler.

The last thing I wanted to do was stand around in a bowling alley. I already stuck out like a hitchhiker's thumb. I figured this would be a good time to ask around, get the lowdown on the scene.

I walked past an effeminate shoeshine boy. He called out to me, "Shine, Mister?"

I looked for the guy I'd tailed here from the Biggs' house. He was just hitting the lanes; he wasn't going anywhere soon. I climbed up into the chair.

"Wow. Nice shoes, mister," he said with a particularly mischievous smile across his young, light brown face.

"Thanks. You can call me Ben."

"Okay, Mr. Ben."

"What's your name?"

"Enrico."

"Pleased to meet you, Enrico." I lowered my voice just enough to match his mischievousness, though not low enough to sound suspicious. "Say, who knows the score around this place?"

He looked up at me as he snapped his rag over my shoes. "There's lotsa scores here, Mr. Ben. Everyone's gotsa score."

I pulled out a twenty and set it on the chair next to me.

"I'm thinking of a guy who might know the big score. You know who holds that scorecard?"

The twenty disappeared in a flash. That's my boy.

"You might wanna go talk to Mr. Spence." Enrico was glancing over behind the shoe rental booth at a solemn-faced man in a sharp black leather cap, the kind with the snap on the front brim that's left unsnapped. "Mr. Spence Nelson. He's the guy that gives out the ugly shoes."

I looked again and saw this particular fellow heading for the bar. Enrico saw me giving the guy the eyeball. He nodded that I'd spotted the right Mr. Spence, then added a little twitch of his eyebrows to make sure we were on the same page.

It's always good to attack in one's natural element. So I climbed out of the chair and set my course to the bar.

"Thanks, my man. Nice job on the shoes. How much?" He gave me a price of three bucks. I gave him a five. It followed the twenty.

On my way to rendezvous with "Mr. Spence," I made a visual check on our friend from Suzi's. He was knocking back his second Budweiser. I don't know jack about bowling technique, but I know plenty about anger. Here was a guy trying to blow off some steam.

Just then a cute little brunette number in a tight sweater and short skirt came over to him and started with the conversation. It was pretty clear they didn't know each other. When it was clear that they were going to get to know each other, I headed for the bar.

The bowling alley bars I remember from my childhood in Las Vegas were not like this beauty: At the Penny's Lanes bar, dim lights reflected cooly off the burgundy leather covering the high-backed curved booths. Smoke hung around in the upper corners. The bar counter had a cushion along its edge wrapped in the same well-worn leather. That edge snaked around the room at random angles, making the bar top look like a dancer's stage at a strip club.

Behind the old lady working the bar were rows and rows of bottles with the prices written on them in black felt-tip.

Possibly the best part of the whole scene was the scarcity of drinkers. The joint was almost empty except for some lush in the back corner, Spence Nelson, another guy with him, and me.

Luckily, this Spence character hadn't ordered a drink yet. Buying a fellow a drink is a great ice breaker as long as you have something to follow it up with. He had just finished talking with the other guy. Neither of them looked like he belonged in a bowling alley. When Spence turned to pony up to the bar, I was in the stool next to him.

"If you're Spence Nelson, I was told I should buy you a drink."

"If I were this Spence Nelson, I would think that I would like to know who this stranger is that so freely offers me a drink."

"I'll give it to you straight. My name's Benjamin Drake, and I'm a P.I. I'm working the Biggs murder. I've been through the standard Q&A regarding this scene. Now I'm looking for some more stimulating conversation that might bring up some points that wouldn't normally show up on a crime report. You want that drink?"

That little old lady bartender was waiting for our order. I told her to bring me three fingers of Old Grand-Dad. Then I glanced over at the man I was hoping could give me some answers.

"I will have a Zima."

A grin broke loose on my face, and knowing that I wasn't hiding it, I decided to ride him a bit: "You actually like that stuff?"

"Yes, I do like that stuff. But more than liking it, I admire it. Zima has character, admittedly a much maligned character, but that is part of the charm it holds for me."

I offered him one of my cigars. He declined, pulling out a beat-up pack of Lucky Strikes from his blue jeans pocket. He was quick with a book of matches. After he lit his cigarette, he held out the flame for me.

"I will tell you some things, Drake," he paused to take a

leisurely drag. "But first you must tell me something."

"What kind of something?"

"Oh, anything. I can judge a fellow by the quality of story he tells. I am not necessarily looking for information that would be perceived as useful. I am through with useful information. I have a Ph.D. in genetics from Tulane, if you can believe that. Now I am interested in the mundane."

I gazed at him incredulously.

"You have a Ph.D. in genetics and you work in a bowling alley?"

"Your first lesson from me: the currently accepted lingo is 'bowling center.' Many people now believe 'bowling alley' to have a negative connotation, as in back alley or dirty alley. As for genetics . . ." This time he paused to drink. "Genetics is a dead end. I procure much more enjoyment from the renting of shoes to eager bowlers; though I, myself, am not a bowler."

This was one Zima drinker I could drink with. But he hadn't provided me with anything but entertainment yet. I discreetly tipped my glass toward the guy I was tailing.

"Let me ask you, Spence, do you know that bowler—"

"You have not given me my requisite piece of trivia. Tell me something, and I will answer your questions."

"All right, here's your bit." I took a moment to gather my thoughts, then I laid this on him: "Four years ago I was on a case involving a man named M.N. Fallaby. His wife hired me because she suspected him of having another woman on the side. Story she gave me had him spending several nights away from their nest with no reason or explanation given.

"So I tailed him. He was a small, bookish man. Funniest thing, he acted like he knew he was being followed, though it was not like he was going to shake me. I followed him to his nighttime destination. And do you know who the mysterious other woman turned out to be?"

Spence Nelson's small eyes, like black marbles floating in heavy cream, stared right through me. "There was no other woman," he guessed. He guessed right.

I continued: "Right. He was alone at the public library of all places. After I watched him pore through books for close to two hours, I went over to talk with him.

"Flat out I asked, 'What are you doing?' I fingered him as the type that, given a reason and enough time, would be able to come up with a yarn to try to throw me off. But if I hit him dead-on, he'd let the soup spill, beans and all.

"Turns out he was an amateur ornithologist and was trying to formulate a theory for the flocking patterns of birds. He was eager to talk. Any of the paranoia I noticed earlier was gone, or at least well hidden, possibly under his slight stutter.

"So after we had been chatting it up, after he brought up how much he loved his wife, I gave him the line on her hiring me to sniff out an affair. I put the question to him: Why not just tell her the truth? I'll never forget his response:

"'I am a . . . weak man. And for there . . . to be danger, there . . . can be no weakness. And for . . . there to be beauty, there must be . . . danger. It's better if my . . . wife suspects me, just enough to thrill her, not ... enough for her to leave. It's the best ... the best way for the ... relationship I'm trying to develop to ... bloom."

"Of course, I assumed he meant his marriage. Thinking back after the case had been filed away, I can't help thinking that maybe he meant his relationship to birds."

I turned away to keep my eye on the dope I was following in the here and now. He was still playing with the brunette. She had her hands all over him.

"Bravo, Mr. Drake!"

Nelson had relaxed his posture now that my story was done. It was his turn to talk. I helped him along.

"Did you know Gentleman Joe?"

"Indeed I did. A better question would be who in this place did not know Gentleman Joe." Realizing that I was looking for more than a yes or no, Nelson understood my silence and continued. "He was one rich bowler."

"Really?"

"The man was loaded. Of course, I place that in the respective context of other bowlers."

"How about his wife?"

A slow, dismissive laughter came out of Nelson's mouth, following a lungful of smoke from his Lucky Strike. "His wife is nothing but a bowling groupie who married."

"There's bowling groupies?"

Before he answered, Nelson turned his head toward the couple I was watching. The guy's game looked like it was improving, he had just thrown a strike. His lady friend bounced up and down, clapping her tiny white hands in quick bursts.

"Why not? I could present you with an extended social theory, but suffice it to say that if you take a group with a shared, specialized interest—add to that money and fame, however relative—you'll find individuals trying to sleep their way up the perceived ladder, like salmon swimming upstream."

"I was asking you about that guy over there, the one bowling with the brunette."

"That would be one Jerry Iverson. He was Gentleman Joe's protégé. A fine bowler with a skill level that comes from more than nightly practice; skill like that, my friend, is genetic. And as you can witness, he is popular with the ladies, too."

Now that I had the preliminary scoop on this Jerry Iverson, I returned my questioning to Gentleman Joe. Even nice guys have enemies, sometimes more than regular joes.

"Joe have any other friends? Any non-bowling friends? You know what I'm getting at: anybody you think'd want him dead?"

"There is nothing, except for the certainty that he is, in fact, dead, that would suggest somebody would want to do him wrong. Gentleman Joe had an enormous quantity of friends. People loved him—especially women." Spence smiled a testosterone smile. "He treated them nicely; that is how he got his nickname. Non-bowlers though, I don't know. He was known to patronize Van Winkle's when he was not at Penny's Lanes."

"The bar over on Cosgrove?" I'd never been there.

"Yes, a lot of bowlers drink there."

A swarthy looking man came conspicuously into the bar and gave Spence Nelson the eye. Spence nodded, almost imperceptibly.

"Now, Mr. Drake, I must take my leave. Business calls."

It was pretty clear he wasn't talking about the business of renting shoes to bowlers. Whatever bad business he was in, it wasn't my business. At least not yet.

"No problem. Thanks for your time."

There was no need for me to get up. I had a good view of Jerry from this stool, and he was still throwing balls with the babe.

Spence made a final comment while scratching the little patch of hair growing below his bottom lip. "That was a good story you told. Were you to ever need some more questions answered, I would be happy to let you buy me another Zima."

I took my time finishing my drink. Things seemed to be progressing for Jerry. After what I figured were about three games, he and his young bowling groupie—I still laughed at the concept—headed for the exit together. I wasn't far behind.

Their trail led to an apartment complex on the West Side of Testacy City. Jerry quickly parked the car in a convenient space right in front. The couple hastened up the cement steps to the building's main entrance. They groped at each other, their smiles acknowledging the awkward glee of the moment. I sat in my car and watched. I was old enough to roll my eyes at their youthful display of lust, but young enough to feel a pang of envy.

An hour passed. My watch said it was only 11 p.m. In contrast to the last case I'd tackled—it was hard to believe that was just the night before—this one held promise. Though I didn't have a lot of details, it was more than I started with, and the getting was easy.

I wanted to celebrate. The drumming of my fingers on the steering wheel got me thinking about my next move. I had just enough liquor in me to want some more. And I knew the place to go.

A call to the Always Reddy Agency from the pay phone on the corner got me a stand-in op. They were sending me Mike Manetti. Truth being the truth, Manetti's not very smart, he's not a helluva good detective, and I don't like the way he dresses. He's okay to have around when you have to rough up a few birds, but when it comes to sitting and waiting, he can't always cut it. Unfortunately, I didn't have time to be picky. Besides, my gut told me that Iverson was in for the evening, and I needed a set of eyes to prove me right. Looked like Mikey's the big winner.

Soon, but not soon enough, Manetti's El Camino rolled up to the curb. Under the light of the street lamp I could make out that he was wearing a grubby T-shirt and dirty jeans. Not really an issue when all you're doing is watching a door all night. Nevertheless, it lacked style.

I filled him in on the situation, told him to watch Apartment 3G (I picked up the number from the registry at the front of the building), and let him know I'd be back in the morning, before 6 a.m. He assured me he had it under control, so I left him to his task and got into my car.

Like a moth I followed the light of the moon. I knew it would lead me to Van Winkle's.

Chapter Seven

WHAT VAN WINKLE KNOWS

VAN WINKLE'S WAS A SMALL, dark bar on a small, dark street. Over the heavy wood door hung a burnt-out neon sign of a bearded man asleep with his back against the stem of a martini glass. A neon "open" sign blazed in the plate glass window. I squinted to get a glimpse inside, but I could only make out a vague sense of movement.

I pulled the door open and entered a crowded, noisy room filled with the bluish haze of smoke and the strains of Sammy Davis, Jr.'s voice in the background. Thirsty patrons clogged the long bar on the left side of the room. On the wall behind the bar, a collection of bowling flyers and pictures covered every non-mirrored surface. A little shelf overflowed with trophies, and a pair of beat-up red-and-blue bowling shoes hung over the antique cash register.

The right side of the narrow room featured a number of small booths occupied by what I'd come to recognize as the bowling type and their groupies.

Intermixed with the typical alcohol advertisements were a number of old-style paintings of Rip Van Winkle. In many he slept under a tree while a group of dwarves cavorted in the background playing a game of ninepins. In others he played a little ninepins himself.

I felt the heat of a hundred eyes as the door slammed

behind me. I licked my lips and approached the bar. The bartender did his best to ignore me. He finally got the hint I wasn't going anywhere and moved my way. Maybe it was the twenty in my fist.

"Help ya?" The bartender looked at me as if to ask me what I was doing there.

"Bourbon. Old Grand-Dad."

A chuckle. "Don't have it."

Damn. "Jim Beam?"

"Don't got that either."

What kind of place was this?

"What do you have in the way of bourbon?"

"Only one bourbon here. Van Winkle's."

"Okay," I grinned, the absurdity cracking my composure. "Give me three fingers, straight."

He went away and came back with the smallest three fingers of bourbon I'd ever seen. And I'd seen plenty.

"That'll be five."

"Kind of pricey."

"I don't set the prices." He took the twenty and headed off again. He poured a few more drinks before I got my change.

I thought I'd throw a few questions at him.

"Did you know Gentleman Joe?"

"Sure. Everyone here did."

"How often did he come in?"

"Couple times a week. Sometimes more, sometimes less."

"He drink with anyone in particular?"

A sigh. "Look, man. I'm just paid to pour drinks. You want answers, you gotta talk to the boss."

"Yeah? Where can I find him?"

"In the back booth," he jerked his thumb over his shoulder as he popped the cap off a Bud. "That's where you can always find him."

I glanced toward the back of the tavern. "Pretty crowded back there. Who am I looking for?"

"Walter Wilson. He's a little guy."

"Thanks." I pulled out a buck to leave him a tip. I changed my mind.

I made my way through the packed club. It was a nice crowd; no one went out of their way to let me by. At the back of the bar, ten people crowded around a large table, listening to a raw-throated voice scratch out a story. All of the listeners were typical of the bowling-type I'd spent so much time around today. All of them, that is, but one. She was a blonde bombshell, the kind you see in the movies. Her skin was too perfect. Underneath her flowing blonde hair she had large, ruby red lips over unbelievably white teeth and blue eyes that held a vacant stare. She wore a black sleeveless top that showed off her ample bosom and a short, black skirt that showed off her alabaster legs.

The storyteller sat in her lap, a hood ornament to the blonde's mannequin. He was a hatchet-faced midget, his dyed black hair, slick with pomade, combed straight back over his skull. His ears were large and grew so close to his head they seemed pinned together from behind. His right hand was missing its thumb and forefinger. I figured this guy for Walter. He talked fast and gesticulated wildly, keeping his audience enraptured as he spun his yarn. I started a cigar, determining that I came in somewhere about the middle.

". . . so Dvorkin steps up to the line, ball in hand. He pauses and looks down the lane. A full set of pins waits for his Smoke Grey Pearl Outrage. He'd just bowled eleven strikes in a row. If he got this strike, he'd have a 300 game. But remember, so far Reado had bowled a perfect game, too, and was riding high with nine strikes."

He paused while he surveyed his audience.

"And Reado was the better bowler.

"Dvorkin began his approach. It was perfect, right down to his follow-through. The ball made a beautiful curve and hugged the right side of the lane, kissing the lip of the gutter. At just the right moment it swung to the left and hit the head pin in that sweet spot. Pins went flying . . . and when the table dropped, there was nothing left for it to pick up."

Walter stopped for a dramatic sip of beer. The entire table followed suit. This Walter had juice. "It was a 300 game, but Dvorkin only got a smattering of applause." Another sip, the blonde kissed the top of his head, then he resumed.

"Now it was Reado's tenth frame. The crowd cheered wildly. He stepped up to the return, rolled his shoulders, and crossed himself—he was quite religious, y'know."

Everyone around the table nodded. They knew.

"He hefted his ball and focused somewhere beyond the pins. Reado had been bowling for a long time, and it was mostly reflex for him.

"His first ball of the tenth was a solid strike. He turned

and bowed to the crowd as they cheered. He wiped his hands, then his ball, and did a quick pray before he quickly rolled another strike—his eleventh. One more strike and it was a tie game.

"Now the way the bet was set up," Walter explained, "the odds were stacked against Dvorkin. If the game was a tie Reado still won. Dvorkin had complained about that, but that's what happens when you challenge a champ.

"Even though Reado was good, he was still worried. He waited for his ball to come up the return, drying the sweat off his hand with the blower. He wiped his face and hands, then his ball. Once more he crossed himself and stepped up to the line, his Fire Red Primal Rage in his hand. He stood a long time, just staring down the lane. When he moved, it was sudden. The ball was out of his hand, moving toward the pins with his trademark arc. It hit dead on; he threw the ball with a lot of spin so he always got great pin action. This time was no exception; those pins were flying every which way—"

"He missed it, didn't he?" one chubby-faced guy blurted out.

Walter pinned him with a steely eye. "You telling this story, Larry?"

"No, no, Walter," Larry apologized, hands in front of him defensively. "I just got excited, that's all."

"Yeah, well, you keep your mouth shut." Walter scanned the crowd for any other excitable types. When he was satisfied that everything was calm, he continued. "Now where was I?"

"Great pin action, baby," the blonde got him back on track.

"That's right, that's right. Thanks, sugarplum."

He paused, taking a moment to recreate the tension that had built up before the interruption.

"Those pins were flying every which way, a strike for sure. We all thought it. Everyone was up, cheering, screaming Reado's name. But someone—I don't remember who—shouted 'Look!', and pointed down the lane.

"And suddenly everyone stopped cheering. There was dead silence. There wasn't a pin standing; not a whole pin anyway. The seven-pin had split in two—right down the middle—and only half of it was up. I swear to God. Everyone in the place just stared.

"Well, they had to get the judges in on this one, and they ruled that Reado bowled—not a 300 as everyone expected—but a 299 1/2." Walter finished his beer in one gulp, slamming the empty mug on the table. The slightest smirk colored his face. The story was over.

"I don't believe it!" Larry cried out, looking around for supporters. He found none.

"Too bad, tough guy," Walter's face was getting a little red, "because that's just how Diamond Dan Reado lost the bet and fell from grace. No one's heard from him since."

Before this Larry could get himself in more trouble, I walked up and tossed a few business cards on the table and introduced myself. I looked at Walter. "You Walter?"

"Yeah, an' this is my joint," Walter laid down his territory. "What can I do for ya?"

"I'm looking into the Biggs murder."

I had the attention of everyone in the place now. It was just me and Sammy singin'.

"Wondering if I might ask you a few questions."

"Shoot," he answered, leaning back against his flesh pillows, throwing his feet up on the table. He was wearing the tiniest bowling shoes I'd ever seen.

"How about we talk alone?"

"These here are all my friends. Anything you got to say to me can be said in front of them."

I knew I had to stir up a little trouble.

"Why would anyone want to kill a bowler?"

I got blank stares as an answer. I tried again, turning up the heat.

"Gentleman Joe was into drugs, wasn't he?"

"You better watch your step, Dick." Walter spat out "Dick" like it was my name.

"I'm just saying that he was chock full of drugs when he died." I heard a few chairs scrape back as angry bowlers got up behind me.

"Now don't be lyin' here. We know Gentleman Joe was clean," Walter cautioned.

"I was at the morgue. I read the autopsy report." Now it was my turn to pause for effect. "He was loaded."

Action exploded around me. I was hit from all sides by bowlers defending the honor of one of their own. Fists clubbed my kidneys and plowed into my gut. A set of knuckles slammed into my jaw, bringing with it the tang of blood. It was good punch. It sent me reeling backward into the bar, where I knocked over a couple of stools and scrambled to gain my footing. Everything went into slow motion. Through hazy vision I saw an angry mob approaching.

My hand had just found comfort in the butt of my Smith & Wesson when I heard a voice shout out: "All right you bunch of jamooks! This is no place for a row!"

It was the loudest voice I'd ever heard, and it was certainly the loudest voice I ever wanted to hear. The crowd turned to look at Walter Wilson standing crimson-faced on top of his table.

"Get back to drinking, or get the hell out!" Walter commanded, his little hands balled into fists.

The crowd reluctantly obeyed. When he saw that the violence was over, Walter jumped to the ground and walked over to me.

"Are you soft in the head or somethin'? I want you outta here!"

"Okay," I rubbed my jaw where I'd been socked. "But I still have to clear up a few points."

A stream of obscenities spouted from Walter. "All right! I'll talk with ya outside, but none of this nonsense about Joe bein' dirty."

"Fair enough."

We went out the back door; the path to the front door was too hostile.

Once outside, I couldn't waste any time showing this little guy I meant business.

"Okay, Walter, Joe was clean. That's the problem. He was too clean. In fact, that whole bowling alley is."

"So you've been there?"

"Yeah."

"You meet Spence Nelson?"

"Well, now that you mention it, I got the feeling he dealt in a few illicit things on the side."

"A few? That boy's got a regular drugstore set up in the men's room! Anything you want, he'll get it. A lot of the boys carry for him. He wanted Joe to help out, but Joe wouldn't bite," Walter explained. "And he's only the beginning of the trouble at Penny's Lanes."

"You mean the bowling alley is a center for crime?"

"No, I mean the bowling *center* is a center for crime." He held up his three-fingered right hand. "Believe me, I know."

I nodded.

"Now you get outta here," Walter shouted. "And steer clear of Van Winkle's!"

That sounded like good advice to me. I hit the road.

I cruised to the nearest pay phone and dialed the Always Reddy office, leaving a message for Rhoda Chang to check on the records of Gentleman Joe Biggs, Jerry Iverson, Spence Nelson, and Walter Wilson. Hopefully I'd have a little reading to do in the morning.

Rhoda is Always Reddy's source for hard-to-get information. Although the Agency keeps pretty extensive records that are shared with other detective agencies across the country, we don't have everything. Sometimes we need police records; when that happens Rhoda magically delivers. We don't know what her private life is like, and we don't ask questions; we like the answers too much.

I hung up and eased on home. My adrenaline surge was wearing off into a somber melancholy, making the pain of my short but thorough beating harder to ignore.

Soon enough, I climbed the steps to my apartment, a small one-bedroom number in a low-profile part of town. No one bothered me here. I flipped open the lock and out of habit took a quick survey; everything seemed to be in place.

I headed straight for the bathroom, where I dressed my wounds and swallowed a couple of vitamins. Then I made a stop in the kitchen to swallow a little Old Grand-Dad before I plopped down in my favorite chair. The table to my right held a banker's lamp and the book I'd been reading: Immanuel Kant's *Groundwork of the Metaphysics of Morals*. The older I got, the more I came to appreciate simple reason, pure deduction, optimistic enlightenment. That's some of what I got out of reading Kant.

I grew up reading speculative science fiction, mostly, although I took to anything I could get my hands on. Included in that lot were plenty of so-called modern writers. I used to be keen on ambiguity and uncertainty, used to think that life's problems were giant structures that required dismantling. Of course, when you tear apart a structure, the discarded pieces pile up and form other, new structures. That's a fancy way to say that when you focus your attention on one problem, others creep up around you.

I realized this after my wife died. I was a fire fighter back then. One night I was going up against a particularly nasty burning building. We thought we had everybody out, but a hysterical woman was crying out for her baby. It so happened that I was going to be the last one out of the building. Well, I'm a sucker for a woman in tears. Out of some sense of duty, I reentered the inferno. Eventually I found the little girl. She lived.

That night, that building, it was the longest I ever worked a single fire. The boys were calling me a hero. I just wanted to go home. I'd play big-shot hero fireman tomorrow after I got some well-deserved rest.

The police intercepted me at my front door. My wife's mangled body was at the morgue, waiting to be identified. She'd been smashed to pieces in some auto accident. The police phrased it more tactfully, but not by much.

I was supposed to have met her for dinner at some restaurant, but she knew I was on duty, and when I didn't show up, she had headed home. Often I wonder: If I had not gone searching for the little girl, if I had let her die, would I have been able to be at the restaurant in time to save my wife?

The answer was probably not to be found in Kant. But his cold, convoluted language soothed my mind, like the post-National Anthem static following a long day of television programming. And my mind, my body, my whole person needed rest.

After all, I planned to be back at Jerry's early. I cracked open the book and read until I drifted off into unconsciousness.

Chapter Eight

SLEEPING IN THE NUDE

MY EYES SNAPPED OPEN just after 6:30 on Tuesday morning. I cursed under my breath; I'd wanted to be back at Jerry's by now. I splashed some cold water on my face, ran a comb across my head, threw on a fresh shirt and tie, grabbed my hat, and hurried out the door.

About thirty minutes later, after stopping for two cups of coffee to go, I pulled my car into a spot a few spaces behind Manetti's El Camino.

I knew I'd find him sleeping. It took two hard raps of my knuckles on his window to pull him out of his slumber. He sat up fast and, though he'd never admit it, scared. He fumbled with the big automatic sitting in his lap before he noticed me.

Relief flooded his face. "Drake!"

"Sleeping on the job, Mike?"

"No way, man. I was just resting my eyes."

"Uh-huh." Idiot. "Fill me in."

He got out of his car, yawned and stretched like he was in his bedroom.

"The chippie left by six. I figured you wanted me to keep an eye on..." he stopped talking, noticing the pair of steaming coffee cups resting on the hood of his car. "Aw, Drake, thanks!"

He reached for a cup, but I stepped in his way. His brow

furrowed. My actions were too much for his intellect.

"It's not for you, Mike."

"What? You gonna drink both of 'em?"

"I could, but I'm not going to. One's for me, the other's for Iverson."

"You got the pigeon some joe but nothin' for your man Mike?"

"It's like this," I sighed. "I'm going up there to play a little game of good guy/bad guy with Iverson. I might have to get rough, and that'll make me the bad guy. The coffee," I pointed at the twin cups, "will be the good guy."

He didn't understand, but I didn't really expect him to. I told him to go home and get some sleep. He hopped in his car and sped off, squealing his tires as he turned the corner.

I trudged up two flights of stairs and stopped in front of the door marked 3G. I set the coffee on the railing behind me and pulled a black leather wallet out of the inside pocket of my coat. I sized up the lock, selected the right lockpicks, and got to work. I wasn't an expert at this, but I was no slouch either. In about five minutes I had the satisfaction of feeling the tumblers roll into place. I grabbed the coffee and slid into the apartment.

It was a typical bachelor pad, a little fancier than most. The living room was sizable, with a huge entertainment center against the far wall. Above it was a wide shelf holding five trophies. Framed bowling posters hung on the other walls. The clothes Jerry was wearing the night before, including those slick saddle shoes, were strewn about the floor.

I set the coffee on the counter that divided the living room from the kitchen and made my way down the hall, past a set of sliding doors that opened onto a balcony, until I reached Jerry's bedroom.

The door was wide open. Jerry was sleeping on his king-size bed, wrapped around a bowling-themed comforter. He was totally nude.

I bent down, lifted the mattress, and flipped it over. I drew my gun. I carry a Smith & Wesson .38 Special Small Frame Model 637. It only holds five rounds, but it's easy to hide and, at this range, has plenty of stopping power.

Getting tipped on his can woke Jerry right up. He sprang to his feet, fighting mad. He extricated himself from the unwieldy mattress and brought his fists up into boxing position. He made a move to attack, but seeing my gun made him back off. Then he realized his goods were hanging out in front of God and everybody, and his attack completely fell apart. The red of embarrassment spread across his face.

"Morning, Jer," I greeted cheerfully. "I brought you a cup of coffee."

"What gives?" he asked, covering his privates with his hands. "Who are you?"

"Let's go to the living room and have a chat." I made an "after you" gesture with my free hand. "After all, that's where the coffee is."

"At least let me put on a pair of pants first," he whined.

"There's a pair in the other room."

The friendly gesture didn't work, so I waved him out with my gun. This time he obeyed.

"Y'know, I used to sleep naked until I started detective work," I explained. "Now I wear boxers, at the very least, when I sleep. Sure, it's not as natural, but that way when someone busts into my house in the middle of the night, I'm not too embarrassed to deal with them. Trust me, you feel much more manly if you're wearing pants."

When we got to the living room, Jerry climbed into his jeans and sat down on his ugly grey-green couch. I brought him his coffee and took mine over to a comfortable leather recliner. I kept my Smith & Wesson in plain sight; you never can tell when a guy might decide to fight.

He took a sip of coffee. "I'm pretty sure you're not here to rip me off—"

I cut him off, snapping with: "Many crooks bring you coffee?"

"No, but I don't get many friends busting in at 7:30 either," he snapped back. "And you still haven't told me who you are."

"Ben Drake, P.I." I sent a card flying in his direction. "I'm investigating the death of Gentleman Joe Biggs."

"Oh," he answered before he took another sip of coffee. "It's a damn shame."

"What can you tell me about it?"

"I don't know nothing but what's in the news."

"I understand you knew him well," I prodded.

"Yeah, he was like a big brother to me. He taught me everything I know about the game. But that don't mean I killed him!"

He was getting defensive. That didn't do me any good;

I needed Jerry to be free with his speech.

"Relax, Jerry. No one's pointing the finger at you." I strategically sipped my coffee. "Know who might want to see him rubbed out?"

Jerry shook his head. "Everyone loved Joe. I can't imagine who might want him dead."

So far all these conversations had been pretty much the same. Everyone loved Joe, no one wanted him killed. Well, I had news for these people: someone did. I thought I'd try the male bonding approach.

"Cute girl you were playing with last night. See her often?"

"No, that was the first time." He paused. "Probably the last time."

"So you don't have a steady girl?"

"What's it matter? They're all the same." He dismissed women with a wave of his hand and a gulp of coffee.

"Same as Suzi Biggs?"

"Joe's wife?" His eyes popped wide, incredulous.

"You know another Suzi Biggs?"

"Guess I only know one Suzi Biggs," he confessed. "I'm just wondering why you'd bring her up."

"I don't think you're that dumb, Jerry, and don't make the mistake of thinking that I am," I cautioned.

"Whatever."

What I assumed to be his everyday bravado was slowly creeping into his conversation. I was hoping this know-it-all attitude would make him careless.

"She and Joe get along?" I sipped from the styrofoam cup.

"Sure. Joe really loved her, y'know. She was his first wife, and he just adored her. I don't know if she felt exactly the same way, though."

"Why do you think that?"

"I got my reasons."

"Share 'em with me," I coaxed.

He paused, thinking it over before he started. "Joe was always kind of self-absorbed. The guy slept, ate, and breathed bowling. And he was always nice to the ladies, but when it came to relationships, they always took second place to bowling … and his mom."

He paused and took in another dose of caffeine. "Sometimes people have other needs, y'know?"

"Are you telling me Suzi was fooling around on Joe?"

"All I know is she's been trying to get into my pants for … seems like years."

"But you didn't go for it?"

"Don't get me wrong, I like the ladies," he puffed up his chest like a rooster. "It's just that I couldn't sleep with Joe's woman. I always thought she was half-joking. Besides, it wouldn't have been doing right by him. Anybody else's wife, sure. But not Joe's."

"When's the last time you saw—"

"Joe? Sunday night at the center," he answered fast.

"Actually, I was going to ask about Suzi. When's the last time you saw her?"

"Man, I don't know. I don't keep a datebook. Couple of days ago?"

"You're lying to me, Jerry. I know you were at her house last night."

He looked to the floor and muttered, "Christ …"

"What were you doing there?"

"I just wanted to see if she needed anything. Y'know, after Joe's death."

"Uh-huh. Fight about anything?"

"Fight? Why would we fight?" The faintest line of sweat beaded his brow.

"I was hoping you could tell me."

Jerry looked away, out across his balcony. He answered without looking at me. "Nope. We didn't fight about a thing. I just wanted to see if she needed anything."

"Did she?"

"No …" his voice trailed off.

I sensed he had something else to say, so I let the quiet sound of the waking neighborhood fill the apartment.

After a few moments, Jerry looked over at me. "So you wanna find out who killed Joe?"

"That's why I'm here."

"You might wanna check out Jack Walker," he whispered.

The name sounded familiar, but I couldn't place it. "Who's that? Some bowler?"

"C'mon, everyone in Testacy City knows who Jack Walker is."

"You mean the ball bearing guy?"

Jack Walker was a bit of a local celebrity. He was the head of Walker Industrial, Testacy City's sole big industry: the manufacture of ball bearings.

"Yeah, the ball bearing guy."

I laughed. The idea was ludicrous.

"That's the best you could do, Jerry?"

"No, really, man, I'm giving it to ya straight," Jerry insisted.

"What do you know that would connect him to this?"

I was still skeptical. Jerry finished his coffee.

"Couple a years back, he and Suzi used to be an item. He bought her all sorts of fancy things, told her he'd leave his wife for her, but never got around to it. Suzi got bored with him and hooked up with Joe. Walker never really could let her go, though, and he's been trying to get her back ever since. Joe didn't know about it. Hell, no one knew about it."

"Then how'd you find out?"

"Suzi told me, man."

"Why?

"She trusts me. We're pretty close in age, we like the same music. We get along."

I got out of the recliner and slid the Smith & Wesson back into its hiding place.

"All right, Jerry, go back to bed," I said, backing out of the apartment. "And for chrissakes put on a pair of boxers."

As I walked down the steps I had to wonder about Jerry. I didn't believe everything he told me. And I think Suzi Biggs left some things out of her story as well. Something between these two was missing.

Jerry's bit about Jack Walker intrigued me, though. No one really knew Walker, except for what they read in the magazines and papers. Everything printed told them this guy was a pillar of the community: good family man, contributor to local charities, member of the Knights of

Columbus. Not the kind of image that immediately brings to mind adultery. But now that the idea had been forged, it seemed fairly believable. Definitely worth checking out.

First things first. My stomach, which had only had booze and coffee since yesterday morning, was telling me it needed something a little more substantial. I headed down the block toward the diner on the corner and a spot of breakfast.

Chapter Nine

LUNCH IN THE COMMISSARY

I DROPPED SOME SILVER into the metal box outside of Hopper's Diner. The coins made the glass door pop open, and I took out a copy of the Testacy City *Herald-Tribune*. My eye caught the Biggs headline on page one. I'd have time to digest it once I'd put some food past my teeth.

Inside Hopper's I grabbed a counter seat. I was barely situated when a young, gum-chewing doll with pink lipstick placed a coffee mug in front of me. I nodded toward the cup. She filled it.

I opened the paper, searched for the page with the crossword puzzle, and refolded the paper into a manageable shape, like I was doing some oversized origami.

Completing a crossword puzzle always brought me a healthy dose of joy. Easy puzzles helped warm up the mental muscle, and the *Herald-Tribune*'s were never very difficult. This morning's, looking to be no great challenge, held true to that theorem. The topic: Entertainment.

The waitress was back. I noticed her name badge: Dierdre.

"Dierdre. That's a pretty name," I told her.

"Thanks. It's the only one I got. You ready?" She had her ballpoint aimed at her pad.

"Steak and eggs, please."

"How you want them?"

"Well-done for both. Eggs fried over hard. Tell the cook I don't mind if they're crispy."

"I'll tell him."

I let the facts that I had about the Biggs case wrestle themselves in my noggin while I occupied my lesser faculties on this joke of a puzzle.

It was hard for me to be distracted by the crossword. Jack Walker's name kept ringing between my ears, and the more I thought about it, the more I believed Jerry's story. It's hard to get that big and powerful without getting dirty—especially in this city. Testacy City was corrupt all right. It took the place left vacant by the old Vegas once the strip became some sick family entertainment complex.

Going up against Jack Walker wasn't going to be easy. Getting information out of him would be like springing a guy from Sing-Sing; while not completely impossible, I didn't want to do it.

Dierdre brought me my plate of breakfast and topped off my coffee. I asked her if she knew an eight-letter word for hairless.

"How about 'balding'?"

"That's only seven letters."

"Then I guess I don't know." She cocked her head in the direction of the kitchen. "Hey, Emil! Word for hairless. Eight letters." She looked back at me. "What's it begin with?"

Caught off-guard and slightly perplexed, I looked back at the puzzle. "Ah, the letter *g*."

"Begins with *g*," she shouted to the cook.

A funny, guttural sound came from the kitchen: "Glabrous!"

I stared at the waitress. She made a loud snapping sound with her gum. "He knows everything. Go ahead, ask him something else. His name is Emil."

I figured it was worth a try. "Hey, Emil. You know who killed that bowler, Gentleman Joe Biggs?"

A funny, guttural sound came from the kitchen: "No!"

Several comments came to my mind, but I let them stay there. Dierdre had already gone off to wait on somebody else. I dug into my breakfast, not wanting it to get cold.

After breakfast I went to the office. One of the worst things about being a private eye is having to get up early. That doesn't fit well with my habit of staying up late. Some mornings I wish I had a 9-to-5. But then I'd have to shower in the morning. This way I can wait until the afternoon. It's a good way to break up the day.

On my desk I found reports on Joe, Jerry, Spence, and Walter. Here's how they played out:

Joe was clean as a whistle. That matched everything I had heard, guessed, or already found out about him.

Jerry was slightly dirty: shoplifting, minor drug possession, driving without a license, disorderly conduct—that sort of thing. This Iverson character was a walking, talking misdemeanor. These petty crimes either belied some larger offense that he was just waiting to get caught at or served testament to a sloppy life. Either way, I wasn't done keeping my eyes on Jerry.

Spence's record had a playlist of possession charges. Looked like the dirt I got from Walter was dead on. I was certain drugs didn't play in this murder. That didn't mean Spence and I were through with each other, though.

Walter, surprisingly, only had a drunk-and-disorderly beef on file from his younger days. That was flat out no help.

I put the last file down on my desk, then looked up at the clock. It was 9:30. Time to call Mr. Walker.

I dialed the main number to Walker Industrial. I got an operator who, when I asked for Mr. Walker, transferred me immediately. That meant I was going to be dealing with his assistant.

Sure enough, a perky non-Jack Walker voice picked up the line.

I responded to this voice: "Jack Walker, please."

"I'm sorry, Mr. Walker is busy. May I take a message?"

"I think he'll want to talk to me."

"Who's calling?"

"Benjamin Drake. I'm a private investigator. I'd like a few moments of Mr. Walker's time to—"

"Hold on." Her sigh, barely discernible, started to drift my way before the line cut off, and I found myself listening to the soothing sounds of Testacy City Light FM. I would have expected—and preferred—a classical station. Adult contemporary never made me happy. I'd use that unhappiness to my advantage.

The assistant returned: "No, I'm sorry, he's all booked up."

"Well, never mind. I just wanted to congratulate him on keeping his name out of the papers—you know, with Suzi Biggs' husband dead and all. Wish him good luck in the future for me." I paused just long enough to see if she'd take the bait. She did.

"Oh, he just finished his meeting. Ah, hold on a moment." She returned me to my Easy Listening. There was nothing easy about it. Thankfully, she came back quickly. "We can fit you in today at noon."

"Great! Are we going to have lunch at the commissary?"

"No, sir. 12:00 in his office."

Too bad, I've always heard the Walker Industrial commissary is top-notch.

"Noon it is, then." I made the receptionist happy by hanging up.

I got down to a little paperwork. I heard a door slam, reminding me that Hal Reddy was always here. I was tempted to give him the lowdown on what I'd found so far, especially since the last time we spoke I had to admit that I came up short on my previous case. But I knew he'd knock me down a couple rungs by asking me if all my information added up to knowing who the killer was. I'd have to admit no. Letting him know all I had was a few leads wasn't worth that. It certainly wasn't worth enduring the stench of his cheap cigars.

Paperwork got dull, and I found myself at Elizabeth Biggs' with a bag of eclairs.

"Hello, Benny! I was just frying up some Jimmy Dean. Can I get you some?"

Oh, brother. I declined the sausage, since I already had

breakfast; I didn't mind helping myself to an eclair, though.

I was there to fill her in. I felt a little strange. A bunch of information had fallen my way since we last spoke, but none of it amounted to an answer. I left it at the simple truth that I was making good progress.

She had been watching television and invited me to join her. We watched one of those daytime talk shows that the night-time talk show hosts often make fun of. Now I know why.

As casually as possible, I asked her about Jerry Iverson. She told me he was like a kid brother to Joe.

"Is he helping you out, dear?"

Iverson was helping me out all right. It was clear she didn't know anything about him and Suzi; if she had, I'd have heard it.

She kept deflecting my questions, either offering me coffee, asking if I was getting enough sleep, or remembering trivial anecdotes from her life raising Joe.

I wondered aloud if Jerry had been to see her.

"No, he hasn't. But so many nice people have sent me cards and flowers. I'm sure his is among them. Would you like to see all the lovely cards they sent me?"

I went through the cards. She was right. They were lovely.

The morning was slipping away from me. I wanted to stop home and run some water over my body before I had my encounter with Jack Walker.

I knew Elizabeth wouldn't mind if I used her phone. I'd save time if I could check my messages at the office.

Since I just pissed off a bar full of bowlers the night before, there was no telling when something would shake loose.

Rhoda told me that Dino from the bowling alley had called a couple of times saying he had something that might help me out. I instructed her to tell him that I'd stop by the alley as soon as I could.

I didn't have time right now. After all, I didn't want to keep Mr. Walker waiting.

Chapter Ten

MR. WALKER

I WAS SITTING in a high-backed leather chair, and I would've been comfortable if not for the two muscles from the Middle East standing on either side of Walker's mahogany desk. I knew they were Jack's bodyguards, but to me, they were pure punishment in suits.

The room was silent.

Jack Walker knew how to keep his distance. My chair sat a good ten feet in front of Jack's desk, and the desk itself was a generous three feet deep.

Behind this distance loomed the curly-haired presence of a man with power. He wore no glasses. His face was clean-shaven, exposing his strong rock of a jaw. His affluent lifestyle provided him with a youthful vigor. It was impossible for me to determine his age, but I remember reading somewhere that he was in his fifties.

The smoke from the pipe he held between his clenched teeth gave the air a rich, woodsy smell. Maintaining the silence, he leaned back in his chair. Through the smoke his eyes were fixed on me, eyes that were deep-set below thick tufts of black eyebrows. Unable to resist the urge, I fidgeted slightly.

He knew what he was doing. Just as I was about to break this verbal stand-off, he spoke.

"Is there something I can do for you ... Drake, wasn't it?"

"That depends." I hoped that by speaking slowly I could mask my uneasiness. "Depends on what you know about bowling. And it depends on where you were early Monday morning, between one and nine a.m."

"Look around you, Drake. Do you think I'm a man who goes anywhere or does anything without a paper trail?"

He made a new cloud of smoke with his pipe; a thin, distinct line rose from its bowl.

"I can tell you I wasn't bowling."

"Nobody thinks you were bowling."

"And what do people think I was doing? Oh, excuse me—what do *you* think I was doing? Let's cut to the chase so I can throw you out of here."

I leaned forward in my chair.

"All right, here it is: having an affair with a girl whose husband shows up dead—that doesn't look too good, Jack."

Not the kind who ruffled easily, he took the accusation in stride. I was more concerned with how his two heavyweights would take it. The expressions on their brown, sandstone faces remained frozen in permanent snarls. They were practically twins: both wore dark suits with purple sashes around their waists like cummerbunds, and each had the hair growing off his chin greased into the traditional upturned jheri curl. I half-expected them to have scimitars hidden somewhere.

"Your proof, Drake? I notice you're not here with the police."

"I'll get proof when I need it. And if you think you keep such a clean trail, then how'd I find out about Suzi, smart guy?"

I eyed the two pairs of Indian fists. Clenched, they looked like jackhammers.

Walker was still playing with me when he asked, "Please do tell me, how *did* you find out?"

"Uh-uh, that's a secret. I'll be in touch."

He waved his hand dismissively: "Get him out of here." He leaned forward to write something on a legal pad. Without looking up he added, "Butch and Schultz will show you to the front."

The Indian muscles moved like robots. I got up before they could grab me.

They came with me as I rode the elevator down to the garage, one standing on either side of me. It was a tight fit. I had no idea which one was Butch and which one was Schultz. I was tempted to ask them about their decidedly non-Indian names. I decided against it, having caused enough trouble here.

Driving away from the Walker Industrial offices, I didn't have much time to think about my encounter with Jack Walker, because I soon noticed a black Lincoln (my guess: Butch and Schultz) doing a rather sad job of trying to follow me. Apparently, I was not going to be so easily dismissed.

I had some fun trying to shake them, but even with their sloppy driving, they managed to stay with me. I could excuse the bad driving; the poor tailing technique was another matter. Obviously, these guys needed a little crash course in the Ben Drake rules of shadowing.

I started to lead them into the maze-like streets of

Testacy City's west-side hills. Before I got there, the fuel gauge caught my eye: the needle was just kissing the E. The last thing I wanted was to run out of gas on some residential street. I decided to try a different approach. Lepke's, a diner I liked to frequent, was right up ahead. I figured I'd grab a bite, maybe get one of the waitresses to set up a distraction for whoever was tailing me, then bolt out of there.

More important though, Jack hadn't bought me lunch. And that left me mighty hungry.

When I turned into the parking lot, the Lincoln quickened its approach. As I scurried to get to the entrance, the big car nearly smashed through the front door in a successful attempt to intercept me. Simultaneously, Butch and Schultz erupted from the car and started toward me. As big as the car was, it seemed too small to hold both of them.

I hadn't expected them to make a play for me, especially in broad daylight.

"What's shaking, guys?" I began walking slowly backward. This was going to be ugly.

"Mr. Walker's got a lot of affairs that are very delicate, affairs that a guy like you could really mess up," one of them said, cracking his knuckles. "We're here to make sure you don't do anything stupid."

With speed I hadn't expected from their enormous size, one thug walloped me but good in the stomach. Then, out of some violent sense of balance, the other one knuckled me as well with a heavy blow upside the head, right behind my left ear. This second blow brought

me to my knees, breathless. My head got all soft-fuzzy, and a high-pitched wail began sounding from somewhere deep in my brain-pan.

"Consider this an advance on a beating to come," a coarse voice rumbled.

When my eyes regained their focus, I looked up to find the gorillas' car speeding away behind a thick cloud of desert dust. It was then that I realized the ringing in my ears was really the droning of a police siren.

I managed to pull myself to my feet just in time to greet the squad car that pulled up beside me. I waved the cops on, hoping they got the message I was okay. They didn't.

Two boys in blue jumped out, ready for action. Too bad all the action here was finished.

"All right, buddy, you're coming with us," the taller of the two said.

I looked around, then laughed, even though it hurt.

Chapter Eleven

POLICE INTERVIEW

THE ONLY THING I could get out of the jokers here at the police station was that Duke Wellington wanted to talk with me. Already, I'd been in the holding room for close to two hours. Various officers occasionally brought me styrofoam cups of what passed for coffee along with a promise that they'd be right with me. Both left a bad taste in my mouth.

Finally, a cop I knew came to see me. Mark Weisnecki, a tall, mustachioed lunkhead of a detective who had the pleasure of being Duke Wellington's partner. I trusted precious few of the police in this town, and Weisnecki was no exception. But at least he was easier to talk to than Duke Wellington.

"Sorry about this, Ben."

"Don't be. Just tell me what the hell this is all about. Better yet, tell me when I get to leave." Raising my voice as I did brought back the pain in my head.

"The main man wants to ask you some questions," Weisnecki said apologetically.

"That's no good, and you know it! I want some answers."

The door flew open, banging loudly against the wall behind it.

"I'll give you answers!" Duke Wellington stormed in, waving his arms, not stopping until he was inches from my face. He was in a dark grey suit, maroon shirt, and a silver tie. The smell of musk pushed its way toward me.

He continued yelling at me, "You want answers? Fast and furious, I'll give you answers, answers with big question marks at the end of them! How about this answer: What in God's good name you doing messing around with Jack Walker?"

"Who?"

I was tired and beat, but I always had a bit of extra energy available to yank this guy's chain.

Weisnecki intercepted, "Ben, don't give him a hard time and then expect us to cooperate with you."

I snapped back at him: "I don't want you to cooperate with me!"

Duke Wellington was pacing the room. He grabbed a chair, pulled it over to where I was sitting. He spun it around and straddled it backward.

"Okay, Drake, let me break it down for you."

He rolled his head on his shoulders as if he were warming up for some exercise. Motioning to Weisnecki with his chin he said, "Mark, break it down for him."

Mark did: "It's like this, Ben. We've been trailing you since you left Iverson's. We know you met with Walker. We know his goons were trailing you."

"Do you know who killed Gentleman Joe Biggs?" I had little patience left.

"No," Weisnecki blurted out.

"Then the truth is you want *me* to cooperate with *you.* Well, I got news for you and DW: I'm not a cop. I don't get paid to help you out, and I'll be damned if I'm going to do it for free."

Duke Wellington's loud mouth went off again: "Are you asking for a payoff, you dirty little…"

"Come on," I said. "This is entrapment!"

Weisnecki continued what he was trying to say, "We know Walker's goons were trailing you. You must have had something pretty irksome to say to him. How about telling us what you were doing at Jack Walker's office and what bit of information you gave him?"

I didn't feel like answering. Even if I did, I wouldn't have.

We stayed like that for a while: Duke Wellington sitting right in front of me, trying his best to stare me down. Mark Weisnecki leaning his hulking body against the wall. Me just sitting there.

Duke Wellington was the first to start up again. "We're not threatening you, Drake. You'll know when we're threatening you."

"Oh, will I?"

"You'll know, you'll know. What we're doing here is trying to cooperate. You and us, see. Cooperate. We're trying to do our job. We're just a pair of honest cops."

I glanced at Weisnecki. He turned away.

I said, "Give me a break."

"What were you doing at Walker Industrial, Ben?" Mark was sounding like a skipping record. He wasn't getting any happier. "What'd you tell him?"

"The fact that you want to know so badly makes me want to tell you all that much less. And…" I pointed at the hothead detective sitting in front of me. "You're the last person I'll tell anything."

He sprang up and tossed his chair to the side.

"Maybe you'll talk to my fists!" He came at me.

I was up to meet him. "Maybe my fists'll talk to you!"

Before we could get to swinging, the calmer detective rushed over and pushed his partner out of the way. Weisnecki then took two fists-full of my lapels and lifted my 180 pounds high enough from the ground that only my toes remained there.

He growled, "Let's get something straight: I don't want to be wasting the night with you any more than you want to be wasting it with us. You're not here to find out what we know, you're not here to ask us questions, and you're goddamn not here to throw fists at my partner."

He put me down, but he kept a hold of me. "You're here to answer a few simple questions."

He walked to the back of the room and leaned against the wall, right next to the "No Smoking" sign. He pulled out his Marlboro reds and tossed one into his big wet mouth. I licked my lips. It was going to be a long night.

"Now, how about telling us what you were doing at Jack Walker's office?"

Chapter Twelve

GIRL TROUBLE

IT WAS LATE when I left the police station. I was glad finally to be out and able to smoke. Smoking made it easier to think. The cops didn't get anything out of me. In fact, I learned a bunch of things from them, the most important being that they hadn't known about the Jack Walker/Suzi Biggs affair. They still didn't.

Another thing: they had Jerry figured as their key suspect, but for all the wrong reasons. As near as I could tell, they had him playing the jealous boyfriend role. I didn't buy it. I wasn't ready to clear Jerry, but he had too many women following him to bed for him to whack a fellow bowler, and a big brother figure at that, out of jealousy.

Spence Nelson's name didn't come up, though they made enough references to the drug scene at the bowling alley. If they knew that Spence was their man, they'd probably be cooking up some cockamamie scheme to shake him down and see what he knew. I had plans to get to him before that. He liked me, maybe even trusted me. He was going to be my pigeon before he'd be one for the cops.

I had enough of thinking about murder for the day. The police detention had left me drained of everything I had, and mighty hungry to boot. My eyes glazed over, focusing on an indiscreet point on the open road as I thought about ways to relax. Maybe I'd fall back in my chair with a tall drink and an LP spinning.

I picked up a pastrami sandwich to go. As hungry as I was, I was so much more looking forward to the alcohol I had waiting for me at home.

Finally I arrived at my door. My tired hand fumbled with the key, eventually finding the keyhole. It was an effort even to turn the lock. I was beginning to feel I should pass on the pastrami and head straight for the cool comfort of my bedsheets. After I flipped on the light switch, I knew that possibility was gone like the darkness in my room.

Suzi Biggs, who'd been sleeping in my favorite chair in the darkness, was startled awake by my entrance.

Detectives come to expect the unexpected, but this … All I could say was: "How'd you get in?"

She yawned casually, like she belonged here. "I flirted with the landlord. Oh Ben, I'm so glad you're home." She said it like it was her home too.

I shooed her out of my chair. She jumped up. I plopped down. The sandwich bag fell to the floor.

I said, "What are you doing here?"

She grabbed a chair, pulled it over to where I was sitting, and in a move far too reminiscent of Duke Wellington's, spun it around and straddled it backward.

"Oh Ben, I don't want to be alone, and I didn't have anywhere else to go."

I wanted to ask her why she didn't go to Jerry's, but a lot of the fight had been taken out of me, so I didn't.

"Well all right, then. Want a drink?"

. "No. You know, I'm not really a drinker. When you saw me yesterday, I wasn't really myself. I mean, I was totally denying Joe's death."

"Suit yourself. Me, I've had a rough day, and I need a bourbon." I struggled to get out of the chair. "After I get that drink, I'm going to sit down to that sandwich I brought home, and you're going to tell me what you're really doing here."

She laughed a light, playful laugh, hiding her mouth behind her dainty hand. "You're so funny, Ben. I like your style." It was such a put-on it made my brow wrinkle with annoyance.

My fatigue must have chased away the subtlety of my expression. As I turned back to her with my full glass, she drew quiet, sensing my lack of patience with her games.

My body found the chair again. I reached for the bag and pulled out the sandwich. On my lap I spread out the white butcher's paper my snack was wrapped in. Before I started eating, I offered Suzi a bite. She declined.

"How about a pickle then?" I asked, my mood lightening.

"No, thanks. How are things going on the case?"

"At this rate, I won't have to do any detective work. All the clues are coming to me. I can barely keep up with them." I licked some mustard off my fingers.

"So do you know who killed my husband?"

I didn't like the know-it-all attitude she was using. I felt my good humor starting to slip away again.

"Not yet. But I do know a good detective secret—and that is to maintain a balance between action and inaction.

If you're a good detective, like me, just the briefest sniffing around will bring the clues to you. So it's not a matter of me finding the killer; it's a matter of the killer finding me."

I smiled a content, drowsy smile. The pastrami hit the spot, but it made me even sleepier. The two long swallows of bourbon mixed with Suzi's attitude made me feel like causing a little trouble.

"You know, Suzi, I was going to ask you earlier—if you just didn't want to be alone tonight, why not go over to Jerry's place?"

I could see her face turn red. "Why would I go over there?"

"You two seem to be pretty friendly, what with him spending the afternoon at your house the other day."

Her face turned even more red as she sprang to her feet, hands on her hips.

"You've been spying on me!" she accused, shoving her face into mine.

She was angry. She looked better that way; it gave her an edge.

"I'm a detective, sister. I'm spying on everyone."

She harrumphed a high-pitched harrumph and crossed her arms before picking a new seat on the far side of the room. She pouted there for a while as I sipped my Old Grand-Dad. The glass was getting dangerously low.

I had the feeling that she was waiting for me to apologize, but that wasn't happening. And since I didn't care if she was there or not—or even if she talked or not—the evening turned into a waiting game. I waited longer.

"So . . ." A dramatic pause. "You want to know what's between me and Jerry?"

"Sure, if you want to tell me. If not, that's no problem. See, I'm going to find out either way."

"You can be a real son-of-a-bitch, Ben."

"I've been called worse. I thought you wanted to talk about you and Jerry?"

"Yeah, okay," she paused again, this time to take a deep breath before she began. "It all started even before I met Joe. I went down to the bowling alley one night, now I can't even think why . . ."

I remember closing my eyes, telling myself I was still listening to her. But I wasn't, and I fell asleep.

Chapter Thirteen

TOO MANY POSSIBILITIES

WHEN I WAS SHOCKED AWAKE the next morning, I was still in my favorite chair. I had been dreaming, and while I couldn't recall the details, I was left with a lingering sense of blood and violence. A result of yesterday's events fueled by a healthy dose of pre-shut-eye bourbon, no doubt.

I shuddered involuntarily and looked over at the clock. It was nearly 10:00 in the morning, and my whole body ached.

A loud ringing startled me. It was a moment before I realized the phone had roused me from my chaotic snoozing. I picked it up. "Yeah?"

"Where the hell ya been?" Hal Reddy's gravelly voice demanded.

"Yesterday was rough," I explained. "The cops needed a playmate for most of the afternoon, and I was it. We were having so much fun they kept me occupied for most of the evening, too. By the time I got back to my place I was too tired for anything but bourbon and bed."

"Don't be gettin' old on me, Drake." His idea of a joke.

"No problem. What you want from me?"

I knew something was up. Hal never called just to make small talk, thankfully. The last thing I needed this morning was the boss making a social call.

"You talked to some joker the name of Iverson yesterday, right?" He was all business now.

"Yeah, why?"

Hal dropped the bomb. "'Cause he's dead—they found him hanging off his balcony with an extension cord around his neck."

"An extension cord?"

"Yeah, the long orange kind," he explained. "You know, the industrial strength ones."

"Sure. Who found him?"

"The dame who lives two floors below him. She came tripping home after the local bar closed and saw Iverson's body hanging in her backyard. Must've woke up the whole block with her screamin'." I could hear a tinge of glee in Hal's voice. He enjoyed the distress of "civilians," as he called them.

"What are the cops saying?" I asked.

"Looks like the initial call is suicide."

That just didn't fit for me. From what I'd seen, Jerry had too much going for him to want to end it all.

"You got anything else on it?"

"Uh-huh. The cops are fingering this Iverson for the Biggs murder. You wanna check it out and see how it plays?" It sounded like he was asking me, but I knew better than that.

"Sure," I said. "I'll get right on it."

"Good. Fill me in later." He hung up in my ear.

I set the phone back in its cradle and began to strip off my rumpled clothes. My mouth tasted like something had died in it, and I was off to the bathroom for a remedy when I suddenly remembered that I wasn't alone last night when I ran out of gas.

My pistons still weren't all firing this morning, and I actually looked around my small apartment before I realized there wasn't any place she could be hiding. Suzi Biggs was long gone.

I dug through the pockets of my coat until I found the notebook with all the information about the Biggs murder. I flipped through it, found Suzi's number, and grabbed for the phone. My guts felt like they were filled with ice water as I dialed. I knew she wouldn't be there, but I had to try. My guts were right on target. No answer.

I dropped the receiver and got cleaned up. Suzi Biggs was heavy on my mind as I dragged a straight razor across my two-day growth of beard. I still wasn't positive that she didn't have anything to do with Joe's death—or Jerry's for that matter—but I sure had a few questions for her, like where she'd got to last night. Her mysterious disappearance puzzled me. Hell, what she was even doing here last night was a puzzle. She was playing with me, and I hadn't even figured out the game.

The way I was feeling this morning I was going to be no good to anyone—especially myself—without a little coffee in my system. There wasn't any in my kitchen. I kept my cupboards pretty bare.

I took a little trip down to the corner grocery and picked up a can of Maxwell House. I knew when I got back I wouldn't feel like waiting for the coffee to brew, so I stopped in the store's deli and got a hot cup to go.

When I returned home I got a fresh pot going, biding

my time by finishing my deli coffee, enjoying a cigar, and doing a little thinking.

I had a few thoughts on Jerry's death. I wasn't buying the suicide story the cops were selling. It sounded like a frame-up to me, and I needed to dig up some solid dirt to bolster my theory. The police sure wouldn't give me anything I could use, and I didn't trust the press. That left one person who could help me.

I got Rebecca Hortzbach on the phone on the first try. We exchanged the cursory pleasantries before I brought the conversation down to brass tacks.

"So, have you gotten Jerry Iverson's body yet?"

"Yeah, they brought it in early this morning." She sounded tired, not at all her normal, jovial self.

"Look at it yet?"

"Just a glance. His neck was broken and he had a deep contusion around it, but that'll happen when you take a dive from a third story balcony with a cord around your neck. I haven't been able to take a closer look. It doesn't seem to be a priority to the cops."

"What's the general thought?"

"You mean what do the police think, or what do I think?"

"Both, actually," I said as I poured myself a cup of fresh-brewed coffee. "Police angle first."

"Word around here is they're calling it suicide."

"And what do you think about that?"

"Of course I'm skeptical, but it's feasible," she admitted. "Apparently there was no sign of struggle in the apartment, no evidence of forced entry. The techs couldn't find a single thing that would suggest anything other than death by hanging. But then again, there was no suicide note."

"Male suicides don't always leave notes, and I knew Jerry well—okay, maybe not that well—but enough to know that he wasn't ready yet to dangle off his balcony on the end of a cord," I said. "When are you going to get to his body?"

"Last night was a busy night, so I'm kind of backlogged down here. Since the police aren't in a rush for it, I don't know ..." she paused. I could hear her tapping her teeth with a pen. "Maybe a couple days from now?"

"I've got a feeling about this. Could you push that up any?"

Another pause. I heard the lighting of a cigarette, followed by her inhaling, then exhaling. "I guess I can fit it in tomorrow. Wanna watch?"

"No, I've got a full day."

I've seen a lot of dead bodies in my day, and I could handle them just fine. But there's a big difference between seeing a dead body—even a decapitation—at a crime scene and seeing the same body being taken apart in the morgue. For some reason, autopsies give me the willies. Plus, they take at least a couple of hours.

"I'd like to stop by when you're done, though. What time do you think you'll finish up?"

"Hold on." The phone thunked to her desk and sat there for a few moments. I heard the rustle of papers before her voice returned. "Stop by about eleven tomorrow morning. I should be just about finished by then."

"Right. See ya then, and thanks."

"Any time, Ben."

As long as I had the phone in my hand, I decided to call Elizabeth Biggs to let her know about Jerry's death. After all, if Jerry was like a little brother to Joe, he was probably like a son to Elizabeth.

She took the news pretty hard and started crying. It hurt listening to her sob.

When she got hold of herself, she wanted to know if I thought the same person killed them both. I told her I didn't know, mentioning that the police thought Jerry committed suicide. She didn't believe it any more than I did. Smart woman.

I promised her I'd visit soon and hung up.

Jerry's death kind of threw me for a loop. That made two bowlers murdered in the span of three days. Testacy City is far from crime-free, but for some reason it struck me as strange that the fix was in on bowlers this week.

All I had to do was figure out why.

I stretched out on my bed and smoked as I turned it over in my head. Compared to the last case I was on, this one was a cakewalk. I'd almost had to dodge the clues as they came flying at me, and now there were just too many possibilities: Jack Walker, Suzi Biggs, Jerry Iverson, and even Spence Nelson all worked into the mix. Sure, I had a lot of leads, but they all got knotted together in the middle, like one of those kids games on the back of the menus at Denny's, only a lot more tangled up. I tried to unravel everything in my mind, but I felt the weariness of my sore muscles creeping into my thoughts. I quit trying to fight it and closed my eyes.

Chapter Fourteen

CRIME SCENE, REDUX

WHEN MY EYES OPENED AGAIN, the sun was just going down. I dragged myself off the bed and stumbled to the phone, dialing the number of the Biggs residence. There was no answer. Not that I expected one.

Now that it was starting to get dark, I decided it was a good time to check out Jerry's apartment. Like I'd told Dino, forensic technicians sometimes get a little sloppy, especially when their days are filled with one job after another. Rebecca said last night was pretty busy. I was hoping that would play in my favor.

Speaking of Dino, it hit me that I kept forgetting to swing by and see him to pick up his "hot tip." I wasn't taking my junior ace detective too seriously, but nevertheless I made a mental note to check in with him tomorrow.

A light purple dusk had just descended on the city, and I wanted to wait until it was a little darker before I busted into Jerry's. So I steered my car onto the 15 and ended up at The Long Mile, the best restaurant Testacy City has to offer.

It's a comfortable place, dimly lit, with deep black leather booths. It's not fancy or anything, but it's dark, it's quiet, and they serve the best chicken-fried steak with mashed potatoes and gravy in the tri-state area.

John Coltrane played quietly in the background as I

strolled through the tenebrous atmosphere of the restaurant, its serenity slowly stripping away my anxiety. I took a seat at my favorite table in the back. Detectives by nature are a paranoid lot. I'm no exception, and this table allowed me to keep an eye on the whole place.

I always liked to come here when, like now, I was waiting for things to happen. The place had a soothing effect on me. While this case might have been easy so far—aside from getting beat up and detained—I'd been doing this long enough to know that whoever's behind this wasn't done causing trouble.

Lynda, my usual waitress, walked up and presented me with three fingers of Old Grand-Dad straight up. Being a regular had its advantages.

"Evening, Ben. How are you tonight?"

Lynda was a tall woman who looked that much taller due to the voluminous beehive of reddish-blonde hair piled on her head.

"Just, fine, thanks. How are you doing?"

"Y'know … same old, same old."

I took a sip of my drink. "How's Tony?"

Tony was Lynda's common-law husband and the bartender at The Long Mile, and although he was a better bartender than husband, he was a good man. He'd done some work for me in the past.

"He's staying out of trouble these days," she glanced over her shoulder at Tony, working behind the bar, "barely, anyways. Wanna hear the specials?"

"Bring 'em on."

"Tonight we've got free-range fried chicken with

mashed potatoes, baby-back ribs with steamed vegetables, or the chef's secret coulotte steak. That comes with a baked potato."

Now I had a tough decision. Only two coulottes could be cut from a single cow, and it was a damn fine cut of meat. But I had a busy evening ahead of me, one that just might involve some running. The last thing I needed was to be slowed down by a 16-ounce slab of meat sitting in my gut. And like I said, the chicken-fried steak here couldn't be beat.

"I'll go with the chicken-fried steak."

"It's good to know some things never change," she laughed and ambled off, scribbling my order on her little green pad.

I lit a cigar and smoked, enjoying the silence around me. Lynda came back with another drink before she brought me my dinner.

I wasn't disappointed in my choice.

After I finished dinner and left The Long Mile, sharing a smoke with Tony on the way out, it was dark enough for me to check out Jerry's place safely. I pulled onto Draydon Avenue and parked a little way up from the apartment where Jerry used to bed his pretty bowling groupies.

I opened the trunk, where I kept a lot of the tools I used for jobs like this. I snapped on a pair of surgical gloves and filled my pockets with a tiny flashlight, a few little plastic bags, and some other goodies that I thought would come in handy.

For the second time in 48 hours I trudged up the steps to apartment 3G. This time I knew I wouldn't find Jerry sleeping in the nude, but I wasn't too sure that I would be alone.

The door was, of course, sealed with crime scene tape. I pulled out my trusty Leatherman tool and sliced through the tape with one swipe. I tried the handle; someone had forgotten to lock the door. My prospects for finding overlooked evidence seemed good.

I drew my Smith & Wesson and entered the apartment, locking the door behind me. Maybe not the smartest move, but since it was the only practical way in and the easiest way out, I'd rather not be taken by surprise. I figured I could always take a tumble off the balcony to the second floor if things got too hot inside.

I did a quick walk-through behind the security of my gun. Once I had determined that I was alone, I began a more intensive search of the place. The report Rebecca got was right—there was no sign of any struggle. The entertainment center, trophies, and posters were still all in place. The place was neat, as neat as it could be, anyway, considering Jerry's slovenly ways. The bed was unmade, but I had a feeling that wasn't unusual at all.

I moved through the apartment, shining a tiny flashlight into every nook and cranny I could find. I even creeped out onto the balcony. Apparently the cord had been secured to one of the metal bars nearest the side of the house and tossed—with Jerry attached—over the railing into the backyard area.

When I finished my inspection, I'd been in the place

about 45 minutes and had nothing. It was risky being here even this long, so I made my way back through the living room.

Right before I reached the door, I saw something on the floor glint off the beam of my flashlight. I got down on my hands and knees and saw, embedded in the shag carpet, about seven small steel balls.

Ball bearings.

I pulled out a plastic bag and, with the help of the Leatherman, coaxed the balls into the bag. I sealed it and put it in my breast pocket.

Then, feeling anxious, I got out of there as fast as I could without making too much noise. I left the door as I'd found it, unlocked, and pulled a small supply of crime scene tape from my pocket to reseal the door before I headed back to my car.

Once there, I returned my tools to their hiding place and removed my gloves, rolling the left one inside the right one, like I'd seen Rebecca do. I tossed them onto the passenger seat so I would remember to get rid of them in a dumpster before I got too far.

The Galaxie 500's engine roared to life. After the strained silence of Jerry's apartment, it seemed abnormally loud. As I pulled away from the curb, I thought about how I'd got in and out of Jerry's place so easily.

It nagged at me all the way to Penny's Lanes.

I don't know why I headed over to Penny's Lanes; I was just following my detective's intuition. I certainly wasn't going to do any bowling. The place was crowded as ever, but it was a late-night crowd. There were no groups of kids on school outings, chaperoned by bored adults. There were no families. It seemed darker and more dangerous at night.

I headed straight for the bar. I guess I needed a drink, and while I can't ever imagine wanting to bowl, I can definitely imagine drinking at this bar on a regular basis.

The bar was a little more crowded than the last time I was there, but I still saw some of the same faces. The old lady bartender was still on duty, and the solitary lush was holding down what I guessed to be his regular table in the back. It looked like he was passed out; his head was on the table atop his outstretched arms, a thin line of drool leaking between his big lips.

Of course, Spence was there, leather cap and all. He was seated in a booth, and it looked like he was making a deal with some shady character who had about as much business being in a bowling alley as I did.

Walter's comments about Spence and his relationship with "some of the boys" came back to me. This deal looked suspicious enough to warrant keeping an eye on.

I moved to a dark corner of the bar, opposite Spence and his playmate. I'd been watching them for only a few moments when they both got up and left together. I slipped out after them, thankful there were plenty of people who chose to bowl at ten p.m., giving me ample cover.

My quarry left through the front door and headed west. I was right behind when I got held up by a gaggle of drunk young folks coming through the front door. By the time I fought through them and made my way outside, there was no trace of Spence Nelson or his dancing partner. I took a quick stroll around the building just to be sure. I flushed out a teenage couple groping each other in the darkness behind the building but came up empty on the Spence Nelson front.

Next time, Mr. Nelson.

I went back in, sat down at the bar, and had a couple of Old Grand-Dads. No one except the bartender, whose name I'd learned was Mabel, said a word to me all night. And all she asked me was: "Want another?"

Yeah, I liked this bar all right.

Chapter Fifteen

NECKING WITH REBECCA

THE NEXT MORNING I made my way downtown to the morgue, keeping my appointment with Rebecca. She came out to greet me wearing a blood-spattered apron and a smoking cigarette. She still looked good.

"'Morning Ben," she gave me a little wave. "Too bad you couldn't make it earlier; it was a lot of fun."

"I'm sure," I drawled. "What'd you find out?"

"Jerry had some interesting tales to tell. Come on back. I'm sure he'll share them with you if you ask real nice."

She led me through the bowels of the morgue to the autopsy suite. She had apparently just finished the post-mortem on Jerry. His body still rested on the steel table, chest split wide open. What I took to be Jerry's internal organs were piled atop one another on a metal table at the body's feet. Looking at the mound of guts and blood, I never failed to be amazed at just how much stuff is inside the human body.

Butcher-style scales were suspended above the table, hooks slick with blood. In fact, blood was everywhere— on the floor, on the autopsy table, even on the chalk-board where Rebecca had scribbled the weights of Jerry's various organs in neat block letters.

The room's smell was overpowering: a combination of meat just starting to rot, vomit, urine, and feces.

"Sorry about the mess," Rebecca joked.

I laughed. "That's all right. I can take it." I could. I pointed at the body. "So what's his story?"

"Okay. He died about midnight, cause of death: strangulation. His last meal was a burger and fries about three hours earlier. *That* was kind of messy."

"Did he set himself to swinging or not?"

"Not on your life. After we spoke yesterday I made sure to pay special attention to his neck. Come here."

I followed her over to the hollow shell of Jerry's body. The vacant chest cavity reminded me of birchbark canoes I'd seen in pictures. She threw her spent cigarette into a metal washbasin, pulled on a pair of rubber gloves, and put on some oversized wraparound glasses.

"Here, put these on," she handed me a pair of the glasses. "Put on some gloves, too." I followed her instructions.

Jerry's scalp was pulled down over his face and the top of his skull had been cut off. Inside it was just a hollow bowl with a cleanly sliced spinal cord sticking up from the bottom. Rebecca caught my expression of surprise and pointed to a glass jar filled with liquid in which a brain was suspended.

"We'll get to that in a couple of weeks, but I don't think it'll tell us anything new," she grinned. "We've got all we need right here."

She flipped Jerry's scalp back over his head. It flopped into place, sounding like a wet chamois slapping against the hood of a car.

"This," she indicated the deep line that circled his neck, "you might guess is from the ligature."

She looked at me. I nodded. "Sure. I'd guess that."

"And you'd be right. But look here."

She took a long-bladed knife and deftly flipped the skin of the neck back. My untrained eye didn't see anything unusual, other than the deep line that ran around his neck right under his jaw. It looked pretty ugly.

"This contusion," she indicated the deep line, "is where the ligature cut into the flesh. It matches the one on the outside of the neck.

"But these," she indicated a series of deep, bluish-purple bruise marks lower on his neck, "were made by a very powerful pair of hands."

A low whistle escaped my lips. "Would ya look at that."

"You know it. You were right again, Drake: Jerry Iverson was murdered," she confirmed. "But it was set up so that everyone wouldn't even think twice about it being a suicide."

As I've said before, it's always good to be right.

"So why didn't we see those finger bruises on the outside of his neck?"

"Any number of reasons, not the least of which is that our boy Jerry here doesn't bruise very easily. Plus, I think the killer, thinking he knew what he was doing—I say 'he' because those were some damn big hands—used some sort of padding and mistakenly assumed that the ligature would effectively erase any sign of his hands."

She took off her gloves and glasses and lit another cigarette. I joined her with a cigar. I could taste the smell of the room in the back of my throat; I hoped a J. Cortès would wipe it away.

"His neck was broken a short time after he died," she said, finishing her analysis. "That happened when he was tossed over the balcony."

My mind was working overtime, sorting out the possibilities. One kept coming to the surface. "Do you think the same guy killed Biggs and Iverson?"

"All I know for sure is that both dead guys were killed by a strong individual," she said.

"There's no way you can connect them?"

If she could, it would make my job a lot easier.

"They were both bowlers," her voice took on a misty quality, like it did whenever she spoke of conspiracies, "but there's something more to this than bowling."

"Yeah, thanks. Guess I'll have to figure the rest out on my own."

"Be careful, Drake. Duke Wellington isn't going to like you upstaging him again. After you uncovered the truth in the Raspberry Jack case, you're not high on his list of favorite people."

"Hey, I couldn't have done this without you. I just had a hunch—you found the proof. You're on his hit-list, too, and this discovery certainly won't do anything to get you off it."

"True, but he's used to me. And he kind of needs me around—who else would do this job in Testacy City?" Rebecca smiled, chin in her palm.

"Yeah. Well. I'll try to steer clear of him," I said. "But he's already got a mad-on for me, so what can I do?"

"I'm not kidding, be careful." I could sense her genuine concern. "I've got a bad feeling about this case."

I pulled into the parking lot at Penny's Lanes and eased the Galaxie into an open spot. For a guy who doesn't bowl, I sure seemed to be spending a lot of time here.

Normally, Rebecca's paranoia doesn't bother me, being largely a result of her fondness for finding the esoteric wrapped inside the mundane. But this time, there was something in her eyes that had me worried. I knew there'd be more death before this case was over. I just wished I knew for certain where to turn next.

I climbed out of my car, the stench of Jerry's body clinging to my clothes. The two cigars I'd had since I left the morgue hadn't done anything to get the odor out of my nostrils.

I walked up to the old guy behind the shoe rental counter—Spence wasn't in sight—and asked him if Dino was around.

He sniffed and wrinkled up his nose before he grabbed the microphone and paged Dino. I could barely hear his amplified voice above the sound of the alley.

"He'll be calling on that phone over there," he pointed to a small alcove about twenty feet away. There were two pay phones hanging on the wall next to three other phones: a red one, a yellow one, and a brown one. None of the colored trio had a dial.

"Which one?"

"The yellow one," he spat, as if I'd just asked him how to score a strike.

"Thanks." I headed over and waited a moment before the phone rang. I snatched it up.

"Whatta ya want?" a voice snarled at me from the receiver.

"Dino?"

"Of course it's me, who do you think…" A pause. "Who is this?"

"Ben Drake."

"Hey! The private dick!"

"Yeah, that's right," I said. "I hear you got something for me."

"Boy, do I ever," he whispered. "I'll meet ya in the bar in five minutes."

"Sounds good." Actually it sounded great. I hung up and made my way to the bar.

I checked my watch. It was almost 12:30. I never really subscribed to that superstition of not drinking before noon. Believe me, if there was drinking that needed to be done at 8 a.m., you can bet I'd be doing it. For me, the "noon rule" was more a polite suggestion. Still, I didn't like to be impolite too often.

In the bar it was me, Mabel the bartender, and the old lush in the back who was, as far as I could tell, always there. I sat at the bar and Mabel poured me a bourbon. I took a sip and felt it burning away at the bad taste in my mouth. I should have thought of this sooner.

Not long after, Dino slunk in and sat down next to me.

"Hey," he whispered.

"What's with all the whispering, Dino?" I asked.

"Shh! Not so loud," he looked around nervously. "Let's go to a booth."

This was already taking longer than I wanted it to, but I

followed him to an isolated booth. When I sat down he slid a greasy paper bag across the table to me.

"What's this?" I asked.

"Evidence!"

Flames of excitement danced in his eyes.

I opened the bag, and sitting in the bottom were a number of small metal balls.

"Ball bearings!?"

"Shh!" Dino hissed.

I ignored him. "Where'd you find these?"

"On lane thirteen, Monday morning," he said. "They were swept off to the side. Are they a clue?"

"Just maybe, Dino. Just maybe."

Chapter Sixteen

BACK TO JACK

I PULLED AWAY FROM PENNY'S LANES and headed for home. I felt dirty and was tired of smelling like a corpse. I was hoping a hot shower would make me feel at least a little better.

On the drive back to my place, the ball bearings kept rolling around in my mind. After my visit to Jack Walker and the working over I got from his goons, it seemed more and more likely that Walker was somehow tied up in this mess.

I ran some facts through my head. Jack Walker was probably the one person in all of Testacy City who really wanted to see Gentleman Joe pushing up daisies. Iverson was killed the same day he clued me in to the relationship between Walker and Suzi. And now Suzi's gone missing. If I were painting a picture, it would look a lot like Jack Walker. Not that I think Walker would be out doing his own dirty work, but another visit to his offices might turn up something worthwhile. In my experience, guys who think they're untouchable tend to brag about how powerful they are. Walker certainly thought he was untouchable, and I was hoping that with the right persuasion he'd go off on a power trip and let something fly.

I parked the Galaxie and trudged up the steps to my

apartment. I entered slowly, not knowing whether I'd find Suzi Biggs there. I didn't.

I got undressed and put my dirty suit in a plastic garbage bag. A little gift for the cleaners.

I cranked up the water as hot as it would go and stood under the scalding stream. It felt good, burning my skin a bright pink and penetrating deep into my sore muscles, doing its best to soothe. I stood there until the water turned lukewarm. After a brisk toweling off, I felt almost normal again.

I put on a fresh suit, shirt, and tie and headed back out to face the rest of the day, stopping for a quick bite at Lepke's before I made my way to the office.

When I arrived, the place was deserted except for Rhoda. I asked her where Hal was, and she told me that he had gone to the courthouse to testify in the Lewis case. He probably wouldn't be back until late.

I hadn't called him yesterday to tell him what I suspected about Jerry because I didn't like to put guesses into my reports. But now that I was sure Jerry was the victim of foul play, I wanted to let him know.

I wrote him a quick note telling him to call me at home when he got the chance and put it in his in-box. Then I left, feeling a little nervous about the prospect of coming down hard on Jack Walker.

After bluffing my way past the main receptionist, I found myself in the posh offices of Walker Industrial, dealing with Jack Walker's gestapo-like assistant, a petite woman with blonde hair, a pert upturned nose, and bright blue eyes peeking out from behind her designer eyeglasses. She wore a conservative tan business suit and a superior attitude.

"I'm sorry," she sneered, "but Mr. Walker's all booked up today."

"I was just in the neighborhood and decided to stop by," I handed her a business card. "I'll only take a minute of his time."

She read my card, screwing up her face as she did so. I got the impression that she wore the glasses for effect. "He has a full schedule today, Mr. Drake. Maybe if you tried calling for an appointment?"

"That's okay, I'll wait," I said, indicating a comfortable-looking chair against the wall, right next to a framed portrait of a stern-looking man in 18th-century attire.

She sighed in disgust, "I told you, sir, he's all booked up."

"No problem. I'm in no hurry." I pointed at the portrait. "Who's this guy?"

The woman snorted contempt. "That's Philip Vaughan," her voice was heavy with irritation.

"And why is he hanging out here?"

"Philip Vaughn first patented the radial ball bearing in 1794," she recited, like she was giving a fifth-grade speech.

"A real pioneer, huh?"

"Yes, he was. Just like Mr. Walker."

"Right," I couldn't help but chuckle.

I sat down and began to peruse the stack of *Popular Mechanics* back issues spread out neatly on the short table in front of me. I read about electric cars, solar-powered airplanes, cryogenics, and rocket-powered jet-packs.

An hour passed. Then another. The woman behind the desk took a few calls, did some typing, and performed some other receptionist stuff. The one useful thing I learned was that Walker was obviously in his office.

I continued to flip through the magazines, encountering articles that were right out of the science fiction novels I used to read as a kid. I wondered if Rebecca ever read *Popular Mechanics*.

I had just started reading an interesting article about superconductors when I was interrupted by a terse voice: "It's for you, sir."

Surprised, I looked up at the secretary. She was holding the phone out to me.

"Are you talking to me?" I asked.

"Yes, sir. Your card says you're Ben Drake, the private investigator. Is that not correct?"

"No, it's correct."

"Then I am talking to you. You have a phone call." She again thrust the receiver at me.

Puzzled, I got out of the chair, took the phone from her, and pulled it to my ear.

"Hello?"

Duke Wellington's loud voice screamed at me. "I had a feeling, since you got knuckles for brains, that I'd find you there! Don't you learn nothin'?"

"Not if I can help it," I answered. "Do you need something? Like a case solved?"

"Very funny, tough guy. The Cat Lady told me about

you keeping the Iverson death open."

"I'm just doing your job, DW."

"You think you're so smart. You think you got all the answers. Let's try this again: What you doin' at Jack Walker's?"

"Not that line again. Did you call to interrogate me over the phone?"

"No, I called because you figure out Iverson was murdered and head straight to Jack Walker's office. I can't help thinking there's a connection."

"Keep following my leads, DW. We'll make a detective out of you yet."

I could feel the heat of his anger burning into my ear. "We're coming down there, Drake. We're coming down. You'd better not be there when we get there, or this time I'll lock you up and forget where I put you." He slammed the phone down.

I handed the receiver back to the lady behind the desk. "Hold the rest of my calls, will ya?"

I stood there, thinking. I couldn't leave yet; I needed to talk to Walker. I had to find out what he knew. I didn't expect him to sing for me, but I could exert a little pressure and take his pulse. Like I said, he struck me as the bragging type. But I couldn't let Duke Wellington find me here either ....

The next thing I knew I found myself standing in the affluent air of Jack Walker's office, and despite my bravado from moments ago, I had no idea what my next play was going to be.

Walker, sitting behind his desk, looked up as his assistant scurried in behind me, apologizing profusely to Jack.

"Mr. Walker, I'm sorry..." she whined.

His two bodyguards, bigger than ever, started to come at me, expressions of what could only be joy at the promise of violence upon their faces. The whole office seemed to shake with their approach. Or maybe that was my heart pounding in my throat. Just as they were about to grab me, I blurted out:

"Ball bearings were found at both crime scenes, Jack! What do you have to say about that?"

As the sentence fell out of my mouth, I realized it was probably the dumbest thing I could have said. I wasn't exactly thinking straight.

The giant closest to me was readying a fist; his twin was right behind him. I winced, expecting to feel a broad pain across my face when Walker's voice, quiet yet forceful, said, "Hold."

Butch and Schultz stopped in their tracks, though they didn't relax. Like trained attack dogs, they were just waiting for word from their master before moving in for the kill.

"I'm...I'm...so sorry, Mr. Walker, he just burst in," the assistant stammered.

"It's all right, Ellie. No harm done," Walker smiled at me caustically. "I think we can handle Mr. Drake from here. You can go back to your desk."

"Yes, Mr. Walker." Her relief was visible. I guessed she'd fallen victim to Walker's ire in the past. "Thank you."

"Please close the door on your way out," Walker

ordered.

"Yes, Mr. Walker." She backed out of the office, closing the thick, leather-covered doors behind her with a soft thud.

I felt the sweat begin to run under my arms and well up thickly under the brim of my hat.

Walker looked at me for a moment, then picked up his pipe from its stand, looked into the bowl and frowned. He struck a match, put the pipe to his lips, and took a few puffs. When the tobacco was burning again, he blew out a few mouthfuls of smoke that rolled about the room like gentle, aromatic clouds.

"Ball bearings, you say?" Walker asked, his voice thick with derision.

I nodded slowly. "That's what I said."

"Hmmmm," he leaned back in his leather chair and looked thoughtfully at his ceiling. "And you think I had something to do with their presence?"

All I could do was stand there. A few responses popped into my head; they all sounded stupid. I certainly didn't need any more help in that department.

"No snappy banter, Mr. Drake?"

Another puff.

"Let me tell you something. I run this ball bearing manufacturing plant. I oversee the production of millions of ball bearings each and every day, many of which end up right here in Testacy City. Do you expect me, just because of my position, to keep tabs on every one that comes out of here?

"Besides, I own the company, not work in the factory.

Do you for one minute think that I walk about the city, committing murders with ball bearings in my pockets? The idea is," he paused, choosing his words carefully, "well, ludicrous."

"Yeah, maybe," irritation and fury began to rise up inside me. "But let me tell you, Walker, this case stinks. I know you're mixed up in it somehow, and no one—not you, not your goons, and certainly not the cops—is going to stop me from finding out how!"

"I don't know what you expected to find when you came here, and I don't know if you found it, but I think it's time that you be going. I'm a busy man."

"You can't dismiss me this easily!" I shouted, jabbing an accusatory finger at him.

"Oh, I can't, can I?," Walker spat scorn. "I think you're forgetting that you're in my office, and in my office I can do whatever I wish. And I choose to dismiss you. Just like that." He snapped his fingers.

"Now beat it. We don't need any heroes here, Drake. You'd better stick to helping Suzi Biggs, playing her part of the widow in distress."

I felt my face burn hot at his barb, "How dare you …" I started toward him, fists clenched.

I didn't get too far. My anger had blinded me to Walker's bodyguards, and for my carelessness I got a face full of fist. A small light exploded behind my eyes, and I staggered backward, just in time to take a blow to the gut that sucked the breath out of me and knocked me into the leather doors behind me. Gasping, I slid down to a sitting position, lacking the energy to look up at the fist that careened off my chin. I slumped into a pile on the floor of Walker's office.

I remember hearing the sound of Walker's voice echo in my ears and being lifted up like a sack of potatoes before everything went black.

When I came to, I was sitting behind the wheel of my car. My head throbbed like someone was taking a mallet to my skull, and I felt a thick crust of dried blood in my nose. I fumbled with the rear-view mirror until I got a good look at myself. Actually, it wasn't good at all.

The face looking back at me was all lumpy. My left eye was almost swollen shut, and there was a deep gash on my right cheek. My teeth felt like they were hanging loosely in their sockets. A black-and-blue flower was blossoming on my jaw.

On top of that I had no idea where I was.

I got out of the car and looked around. After I took a moment to learn how to walk again, I found that I was parked just off a deserted stretch of road.

The nice thing about the desert is that when you're deep in its darkness, city lights are easy to spot—if you're near any. Thankfully, I was. It just so happened that the lights of Testacy City shone brightly to the southeast.

The keys were in the ignition, so I started up the car and began to drive back to town. About twenty minutes later I drove past the famous "Welcome to Testacy City: Diamond of the Desert" sign.

I stopped at the first liquor store I found and picked up a fifth of Old Grand-Dad. If I ever needed a drink, I needed one now.

I headed for home, thinking fondly of my bed and cursing myself for my stupidity with Jack Walker. I had let my anger get the best of me—and let me tell you, that's the surest way to failure. The crack he made about Suzi still burned hot in my brain.

I was about halfway home when suddenly a crazy notion took over. I squealed a U-turn and headed back toward the highway.

I knew no one was answering the phone at the Biggs residence, but I was hoping that if I staked out the place I'd get a lead or two on what had happened to Suzi. It was too early for me to be jumping to conclusions, but I was doing it anyway. Rebecca's paranoia must have been rubbing off on me.

I rolled past the gates into Victory Gardens and drove up to 300 Pine Lane. The small house looked positively sinister in the shadows of the night. I parked a little way down the street, in the dark space where the light from the street lamps didn't quite reach.

Suzi first gave the impression of a spoiled gold-digger with a sense of entitlement. Conceivably, she could have had an active hand in Joe's murder, especially considering her indifference the day I met her. But with her visit to my apartment, I started to see through her act. Now, given the apparent foul play surrounding Iverson's death—and, especially, her current disappearance—it's likely that Suzi's involvement in this mess may get her killed.

The thought of her turning up at the morgue made me

shudder. Too often I've befriended a person who'd later turn up dead. Seeing the cold body of someone you know is never easy. Even thinking about it isn't easy.

This kind of thinking always made me thirsty. I tore the seal off my new bottle of bourbon and took a slug. It tasted good. It felt good. I took another.

I don't know how long I sat there, but it was a long time. I didn't see a thing. No lights came on in the little mansion, and I didn't hear any sounds coming from inside.

When my bottle was more half-empty than half-full, I started up the car and drove home, smoking a cigar on the way. I don't know how I made it without wrapping the Galaxie around a telephone pole. I was relieved when I turned off the ignition, still in one piece.

I was not relieved when I opened the door to my apartment and found Duke Wellington and Mark Weisnecki watching my television.

"Drake, you gotta get yourself a bigger TV," Duke Wellington chided. "This 13-inch black-and-white is no good. If you're gonna make us come to your house to roust you, least you can do is have a decent TV."

I ignored him.

"And get cable, man," he continued. "This late-night stuff is just crap. You need cable for some good TV."

"You look like hell, Drake," Weisnecki said.

"Observation skill get you that detective job, Weisnecki?" I slurred, leaning against the wall by the door. I needed it to stand.

"Cool it, wise guy," Weisnecki cautioned, raising his lips over his teeth like an angry dog. "You're drunk, so I'll be easy on ya. But another crack like that, I'm running you in."

"Just get out of my place," I said, trying to sound threatening.

"A night in the drunk tank might do you some good," Weisnecki threatened back. His came out with the conviction mine lacked.

"Look, believe it or not, Drake, we're here for your own good," Duke Wellington explained, nodding his head. "That's right, your own good."

I snickered. "Sure. Like I believe that."

"Really, Drake. Let me tell you about it," Duke Wellington insisted. "Mark, tell him about it.

"We're here to warn you to lay off Jack Walker," Weisnecki explained. "For your own good."

Again I had to snicker.

"Just look at you," Weisnecki continued. "You're a mess."

I couldn't argue with that.

"A damn mess," Duke Wellington emphasized. "A damn mess."

"Look, I don't need your help," I shot out.

"Yeah, you can get beat up all by yourself," Weisnecki said.

They got up from their chairs and headed for the door.

"Stay away from Walker," Duke Wellington stopped in front of me, accosting me with a thick finger. "Stay away, or you're going to be in a world of trouble."

"And lay off the booze," Weisnecki said as he walked by me. "Get some help, Drake."

I was glad when they left. I stumbled to my bedroom and collapsed on the bed. I fell asleep thinking that I was going to be damn sore the next morning.

Chapter Seventeen

ELIZABETH'S OFFER

I WOKE UP SLOWLY, FITFULLY from a dark dream. I dreamed of a schoolhouse on fire, a group of young school girls running, their arms outstretched, toward me. They were crying and screaming. All I could make out was the distinct cry of "Help me!" I was just standing there, helpless, feeling like a ghost.

I didn't wake suddenly; my swollen eyes merely opened themselves to the darkness of my small bedroom. My temples beat against my poor skull. I tried to think of absolutely nothing.

What crept into my head was a line I'd read somewhere about a guy who questioned whether we should pay attention to dreams and whether they could be interpreted. The response was that we should pay attention to everything, because everything can be interpreted. Well, the most important thing about interpretation is that you can resist it.

I had to get some coffee in me. This was the kind of morning when I actually thought about grabbing some hair of the dog. But I had that sticky taste of alcohol on my tongue, and I wanted it off.

My breaths came quick and heavy, my eyes were full of paste. When I walked into my kitchen, she scared the hell out of me.

For the second time, Suzi Biggs was waiting for me in my own apartment. My headache got worse.

"Jesus! What in hell are you doing here?" My mind attempted to catch up with what my eyes were seeing. Then I had a bad thought: "Please don't tell me you've been here the whole time."

"No, I haven't. I've been hiding out. Ben, I'm afraid for my life," she blurted out. She was hunched over my kitchen table. In both her hands she clutched a paper cup of coffee from one of those gourmet joints.

"Still friendly with the landlord?" I guessed at her method of getting in here.

"No . . . I mean . . ." It took her a moment to figure out what I was really asking. "You left the door unlocked." She tried a small smile. I could see a lot of the game had gone out of her.

"I don't want to hear any more until I get some java in me. And then I want to hear it all." I moved toward the coffee maker, then turned back to her, adding, "It's a good thing I don't sleep in the nude." She didn't get it. I didn't expect her to.

After I got the Maxwell House brewing, I sat down across the table from her. Suzi wasn't looking at me; she had her head down. I figured I'd give her a moment or two to begin.

She looked up at me and said, "Do you want a sip of my coffee, Ben, while you wait for the new pot?"

I don't know what the hell I was thinking when I took her cup and put the fancy plastic lid to my lips. The moment the sickly sweet liquid hit my taste buds I knew that I should have known better.

"Aaaak, I thought you said this was coffee!"

"Oh, I'm sorry, Ben, I forgot. I have this made special for me. It's coffee that's brewed with the same Indian spices they use to make Chai. And then I have them put in condensed milk on top."

She put her hand over mine. I pulled it back.

"Is that what all the kids drink these days?"

"Is that what I am to you, a kid?" She looked hurt.

Actually, she looked pretty cute. She was wearing a black knit cap over her curly hair. She didn't have nearly as much makeup on as she had the last couple of times I'd seen her. It made her face look younger.

I shook my head. It hadn't stopped throbbing. I had to remember who I was dealing with. "Look, you've played me like one of your boy-toys since I first came across you. You've lied to me, you've played dumb at me, you've tried your damn best to hide behind flickering eyelashes and those big red lips." I felt I was losing my cool, but a hangover combined with a conniving woman in distress will do that to you.

I continued at her: "I've spent the last couple of days getting sucker-punched by bowlers, bodyguards, and coppers. I'm about through with your girl games. You're going to start giving it to me straight, sister, and you're going to start right now!"

Suzi stood up. She beat the table with her tiny fists. Tears were welling in her eyes.

"You probably think I know who killed my husband. Well, I don't!"

She ran to the other side of the kitchen and hid her face in the corner. I could hear her sobbing.

She craned her head around to me. "I saw a big monstrous guy go into Jerry's the night he was killed ... yes, I said killed. Jerry Iverson was murdered!"

"I already know that. And if you want the killer, better come clean and tell me everything else I should know that you haven't already told me. How about you start at the beginning."

I poured myself a cup of real coffee before I sat back down. Then it was time to smoke. I grabbed an open tin of J. Cortès that sat on the divider between my kitchen and what was supposed to be the dining area of my main living space. Here's what Suzi had to say:

"Joe knew how to make me feel ... I don't know, really special. He adored me. And I loved him for it."

As she paused, her eyes darted around the room.

"But I got bored with his bowling. Okay, I hate to admit it, but it's bowling, for God's sake! How can you take something like that serious? I mean, please don't tell me you're a bowler, Ben. Are you?"

"Ah, no. I'm not a bowler. I'm a detective."

"Of course you are, Ben. Of course you are."

She smiled, but when I didn't smile back she continued. "So I started ..." She was tracing little circles on my table with her finger. "... I started seeing what kind of attention I could get. You know, from other boys ... I could get a lot of attention."

"How much attention could you get from Jerry Iverson?"

She laughed a playful, carefree laugh, but then quickly became ice cold. It was as if she suddenly remembered something—perhaps the fact that Iverson was dead.

Her brow was heavy, and she crinkled up her lips. She was thinking about something. A moment later a cute half-smile returned to her face. "I liked Jerry. Not 'liked him' liked him. I just liked flirting with him 'cause he was kinda cute and I could always break his cool."

"The way he told it," I countered, "made it seem like you were hot to get together with him and he had to cool you down."

She laughed so hard I thought she was going to fall out of her chair. "Oh Ben, Ben, Ben, you silly. That's such a guy-thing to say. If he told you that, he didn't want you to know that he never had a chance with me."

"Is that why he was at your place that first day I met you? Is that why you were going to his apartment the night he was given a twenty-foot orange necktie?"

"He was at my place because, because he wanted to ask me something...Oh, Ben, I was in no mood to play with Jerry! He wanted something from me...and I had nothing to give!" She was getting hysterical.

"Calm down."

I had little patience for hysterics, especially on a morning like this.

"And I went to see him the other night because...I didn't know where to turn or who to go to. I tried to come to you, but you fell asleep. I told you I don't know who killed Joe, but I think it's pretty plain that it wasn't an accident!" She wasn't listening to me; in fact, she was up from the table waving her arms about like a mad woman. "I went to see Jerry because I ... I think ... maybe he ..."

"Out with it." I said, hoping for something with more meat than melodrama.

"I don't know! I don't know! Drugs? Gambling? You know how crooked this city is, Ben. It could have been anything!"

"What are you talking about? You saying that Iverson had a hand in this bad business?"

She slumped back down into the kitchen chair, the hysterics gone from her. "I just don't know, Ben. I don't know what Jerry had got himself into. It was something bad—bad enough to get him killed."

The phone rang. I debated not answering it, but Suzi was staring at me with an aren't-you-going-to-answer-it look. So I did.

"Yeah, Drake here."

"Let me get something straight: do I pay you to be a detective or just to run around this city causing trouble?" It was Hal. And though he usually delivered his lines with a pinch of playfulness, there was none of that now.

"Hal, you're one of the main people who taught me that being a good detective meant stirring up some trouble sometimes. You got a specific bit of trouble in mind?"

"You're damn right I do. Police tell me you're busting into Jack Walker's office like some crazed vigilante. Problem here is you're not some vigilante, you're one of my men! I don't give a lazy rat's tail if you want to turn up the heat on some bowling loser, but you turn the heat up on a guy like Walker, ya know whose rump gets roasted? Mine, damn you!"

I pinched the bridge of my nose between my thumb and forefinger as I squeezed my eyes shut. I wasn't used to Hal not backing me up. Letting him down crushed my spirits.

"Hal, I know I acted, well, rash . . . But I got some information—"

"I don't care if you got a photo of the Pope, the President *and* Jack Walker all holding bowling balls over the body of Joe Biggs, let me tell ya what I got for you: this case is closed."

"What!?"

"You heard me. The Always Reddy Detective Agency is dropping the Biggs murder. The whole thing is getting way too political for us, now that ya dragged Walker into this. The police aren't happy about that. And quite frankly, I wouldn't give a good goddamn about the police, but the old Biggs broad isn't giving us enough dough for me to want to throw the finger at the cops."

"Hal . . ." I didn't know what to say.

"Save it, Drake. Take the day off, then come in tomorrow. I'll have a new case for ya. Besides, it sounds like ya need to sober your sorry self up." He slammed the phone down.

Suzi was wearing a frown of sympathy. "Are you okay, Ben? Is there a problem?"

"Yeah, there's a problem. I think the fact that you're Jack Walker's slut has something to do with this murder, and him throwing his weight around has got me—"

She slapped me harder than any girl had ever slapped me. And I'd been slapped plenty hard by plenty of girls.

"You bastard! Yes, I had an affair with Jack Walker, but that was before I met Joe. I have never been unfaithful to Joe! I might be young, I might have done some bad things in my life, but I am not a slut! How could you, Ben? I thought you could help me! All I wanted was your help. I hate you, Ben Drake! I really hate you! You're no hero."

I stood and yelled: "I never said I was a goddamn hero!"

She ran crying into my bedroom and slammed the door shut. I could hear her loud sobs through the door. Christ, I felt like a stranger in my own home. One thing was certain; I wasn't about to just sit there and listen to her cry.

I picked up the phone to call Elizabeth Biggs. I don't know if Hal or anybody else at the Agency had bothered to call her, but I figured it was my duty to talk with her either way.

Being hung over, beaten up, fired from my case, and verbally belittled by Suzi Biggs must have all added up to scrambling my brains if I thought for a moment that calling Mother Biggs would be better than just sitting here.

She knew right away something was wrong; I've said before she was a smart woman. When I told her the news, she cried and cried.

Now I had girl tears in stereo.

Just when I thought I had all the surprises I could take this crazy morning, Elizabeth threw this ringer my way: "Benny, you have to help me! Please, I know you're the

only man who can put this nasty business to peace. I'll …
I'll pay you personally to handle this."

It was the kind of offer that could only spell trouble. I'd
be working outside the law, and I'd be working outside
the rules of my job. It would mean me boiling down
everything to the very essence of who I was.

I was a detective. A damn good detective.

I told her I'd do it.

If I was going to go underground, I would need some
help. And I knew just the shoe-renting geneticist I
needed to recruit.

Chapter Eighteen

BEAUTIFUL YET DANGEROUS

I FIXED MYSELF SOME FRIED EGGS while I let the pain in my head melt away to steel resolve. The best plan in approaching Spence Nelson had me showing up at the bowling alley near dark, which was fine with me because I wasn't about to leave Suzi crying in my bedroom.

The pressure of two murders was wearing her down, but she was still holding back. With a couple cups of coffee in me I realized the mistake I'd made with her: she was just starting to trust me enough to unburden her soul. I had to regain that trust. And I had until evening to do so.

I cracked open my bedroom door. Suzi was curled up in a fetal position, staring wide-eyed at me.

"I'm sorry I yelled at you, Suzi. I had some bad news from my boss come down on my head like one of those 500-pound Acme weights you see in the cartoons. I took it out on you. That wasn't fair.

"I've also spent too much time thinking about my needs and not enough thinking about what you were going through. I'll tell you something. I lost my wife in a car accident. You're handling this a helluva lot better than I did."

A smile found its way onto her sad face. I knew she wasn't the type to stay mad at me for long.

"So, Suzi…It seems I've found myself with the afternoon

off. Want to go grab a bite to eat, maybe get some fresh air?"

She sat up looking as though she hadn't cried a single tear. "I'm not really that hungry, but I do have a crazy idea if you're up for it."

"I'm probably up for it, and I'd be shocked if it was anything less than crazy."

"Let's go see the animals at the Wild Animal Reserve!"

The Wild Animal Reserve was what passed for a zoo for the people of Testacy City. Located about fifty miles south of the city (and almost the same distance from Las Vegas) it was mostly large expanses of natural habitat for the captive animals to run free in, though it was much smaller than the park it was based on north of San Diego.

I thought the drive there and back might be just the retreat I needed to cleanse my mind.

"Okay," I told her. "Let's go see the animals."

"We'll take my car! I just love to drive the desert highway!"

She should have said she loved to drive the highway like a demon shot out of hell. I was strapped into her white convertible Mustang, hand clamped down on my hat, wondering if I'd live long enough to solve her husband's murder. We were racing past the desert sand so fast I thought it would turn to glass.

On top of that, she insisted on playing me tape after tape of her favorite music. Every time I cringed at the onslaught of sound she sent my way, she would eject the cassette, throw it to the back seat and try again. "Oh Ben, that song wasn't you at all. But listen to this. You'll just love this!"

Once we were in the park, she took my hand and started running, screaming, "I want to see the tigers! I want to see the tigers!"

The reserve's star attraction was its pair of Siberian tigers. If I was here to win points with Suzi so she'd tell me her secrets, I was in luck. I happened to know the head animal keeper, a jake I'd met after the boa constrictor snakenapping I'd worked a couple of years ago.

We got to the ledge that overlooked the tigers' habitat and waited only a few moments for my man, Bobby Regardie. He was a tall, lanky gent wearing a pair of blue-green coveralls with "Bobby" sewn in gold stitching on his left breast. His curly brown hair sprouted wildly beneath the matching cap on his head. I made the introductions.

"Hi there, little lady!" His watery brown eyes sparkled brightly at Suzi.

"Hello, Bobby—I can call you Bobby, can't I?" She beamed.

"Sure as sunshine you can!"

She put her arm around him. "I was just telling Ben how much I love tigers, especially Siberian tigers."

"They are wonderful animals, aren't they? So beautiful," he dropped his voice to a whisper and bent close to Suzi's ear, "yet so dangerous."

Suzi gave a little start, her face a mask of mock fright solely for Regardie's benefit. He continued in his normal voice: "They were almost made extinct, you know. D'ja know that there, Suzi-Q?"

She blushed, giggled, and pushed him away coyly. "Oh

you. Of course I knew that. I know lots of facts about tigers. I know there are three reserves for Siberians in Russia. I've always wanted to go to Russia and see them."

"Righty-right you are! There's the Sikhote-Alin, Lazovsky, and Kedrovaya Pad Reserves. Wowie, you're pretty *and* smart. Hey, Ben, she's a keeper!"

I tried not to laugh. "Yeah, a real keeper."

"Bobby! I just thought of something!" She was working her eyelashes on him. This would be good. "Do you think I could . . . I mean, do you think you could let me . . . pet one of the tigers?"

"Re-he-hur-hur-hur," he laughed. He was a strange man. "You see, you see, you don't just, you don't just go up and 'pet' the animal." When he said the word "pet" he made invisible quotation marks in the air with his spindly fingers. "They're deadly killers, you know."

"Yeah, I know." She was bummed. "Deadly killers."

All in all, the trip south did what I had hoped it would: now Suzi seemed to really trust me. Several times on the trip back to the city, she would reach over and rub my shoulder or pat me on the knee. It made me uncomfortable, but I kept telling myself it was for the good of the case.

Once we were back at my place, I wanted to try to start in with my questions, but the sun was getting low in the sky, and I was itching to talk with Spence Nelson. I told Suzi I had to go out, that I'd only be gone an hour or two at the most. Then I told her I'd take her out to dinner.

But first I made her promise to stay put in my apartment; I didn't want to lose track of her again, not when I was this close. Only when she agreed not to stray anywhere until I got back did I leave, making sure to lock the door behind me.

After riding in the Mustang, it was good to get back into my Galaxie. It wasn't as comfortable as Suzi's car, but it felt like home. That and a cigar soothed my mind, readying me for another foray into the dark world of the bowling alley.

Chapter Nineteen

SPENCE'S PARTY

I found Spence Nelson in the bar of Penny's Lanes, talking to an unwholesome-looking lady with dirty blonde hair. He was dressed in jeans and a leather vest, one that matched his ever-present cap. She was a rail-thin girl who looked older than she probably was. She wore a short, grimy floral-print dress and low-top Chuck Taylors with no socks.

She said something I couldn't hear, and Spence nodded in return, rubbing the growth of hair on his chin. She hopped off her barstool and made a beeline for the bar's exit, leaving Spence sitting all alone.

He wasn't alone for long. I joined him and pointed at his glass. "Hey, Spence Nelson. Your glass is looking a little empty."

"Ah! Benjamin Drake, ace private investigator. My glass may be empty, but my soul overrunneth. What brings you down to this bowling establishment on such a fine evening?"

"Let's just say I'm looking for help."

"Intriguing. And am I to assume that I can be the provider of said assistance?"

I blew out a big breath of air. "Well, that's what I'm hoping. I'm still trying to find out who killed Gentleman Joe, and I've run into some … trouble with the law."

"And what is your rationale for approaching me with this dilemma?"

"Look, I know you're not exactly Mr. Clean when it comes to dealing with the authorities ..." I trailed off, hoping he'd get the point. He didn't let me off that easily.

"And you are looking for 'Mister Clean'? I am certainly not this Mister Clean, nor do I know his whereabouts. I will tell you, though: if, instead, my likeness were to be placed on bottles of cleaning supplies, many more units would be sold."

I liked Spence's humor—at least I did the first time I talked with him. This night, though, my capacity for his brand of absurdity wasn't nearly that high. "Cut the shtick. I was making a point, and you damn well know it."

He slid his shoulders back away from me, lowered his chin to his chest, and said through down-turned lips, "Just what is the point you are trying to make?"

"It's that I know that your business—and I'm not talking about bowling shoes—puts you on the side of the law that cops don't like. There's a lot of talk at the station about drugs being involved in this case." I leaned in closer. "And that means you."

He stared blankly at me.

I continued what I had to say: "Now, I know and you know the cops are barking up the wrong tree. I also know you've got more secrets about this 'bowling center' that haven't made their way to my ears. It's high time we had a real talk. Here, let me tell you what I know ..."

"I already know what you know," he interrupted.

"So you know that I'm officially off the case?"

"No," his eyes popped ever so slightly in surprise. He licked his teeth. "I did not know that."

"Well, I am. But despite that small setback, I'm still going to find out who killed Joe Biggs—and Jerry Iverson. I think you can help me."

"Of course, I can help you," Spence confirmed. "In fact, I have already made up my mind as to whether or not I *will* help you. But first, tell me why you think I would lend you assistance."

I paused and collected my thoughts. I needed his help, and from what I'd seen of him so far, I'd figured that I'd only have one chance.

"It's my gut feeling that despite your dalliances into the realm of illegality, however minor," I emphasized, pulling out all the stops, "you have what Kant would call a *duty* to what is right."

". . . to *do* what is right," he laughed. "You have not yet failed to surprise me, Drake. I had already made up my mind to assist you, but after your use of Kant as a rhetorical tool, I will do so with zeal."

"I'm glad," I breathed a sigh. "So you want to get to it?"

"In a moment. First, I have to finish a business transaction. It should not take more than five minutes of my, and likewise your, time."

"I'll be waiting right here, then we can get down to business of our own."

He walked off, heading toward the men's room, no doubt. I turned to the bar, signaling Mabel to pour me a drink.

"Say, Drake," Spence called to me from the door of

the bar.

"Yeah?" I asked, turning around to look at him.

"I am willing to say that this partnership shows great promise," he stated.

"Yeah, I think so, too," I laughed. "Just like Frank and Jesse James."

He laughed in return and disappeared from the doorway.

Mabel brought me a fresh bourbon. I lifted it to my lips, anticipating the sharp sting on my tongue. But just as I was about to drink, something stopped me. It was something that, while not unusual in and of itself, was strange and unexpected:

The lush who always occupied the back corner of the bar stood up.

This was the first bit of movement I'd seen out of him all week, and near as I could tell he drank more than I did. He moved across the bar with a strong, confident walk that was anything but the walk of a drunkard. Even though the bar was dark, when he got close to me I noticed that he wasn't as old as he looked from a distance. He had a strong jaw and thick muscles in his neck. He continued strolling, right out of the bar.

I wasted no time in following him. Something was wrong, and I had a bad feeling it had to do with my new partner in crime.

I left the bar and noticed that the few people who were bowling this afternoon weren't bowling now. Instead, all eyes were on the cops—both uniforms and detectives—heading toward the men's room.

I heard a voice shout: "Okay, Nelson, give it up! We've got the place surrounded."

I wouldn't have been able to hear Spence's reply even if there were one. I assumed that he didn't answer, because just then a group of cops showed up with a battering ram and proceeded to knock the door off its hinges.

I couldn't see into the restroom, so I didn't know what was happening until two cops dragged out the dirty broad in the floral-print dress Spence had been talking to when I arrived.

"He jumped out the window!" she screamed hysterically. "The window!"

"Who was on the window?" one of the detectives yelled out.

I didn't wait for an answer; knowing the Testacy City Police, I was willing to bet no one had been watching that window. I ran as fast as I could for the exit. I still needed Spence's help; I had to get to him before some too-eager rookie cornered him.

The bathroom window overlooked the parking lot, so I assumed that's where all the action would be taking place. I burst through the door into the cool evening air and paused. I could hear the sound of gunfire. I drew my gun. It sounded like there was a party, and I didn't want to be caught without any favors.

I ducked behind the cover of a nearby car to assess the situation. About ten cops had Spence cornered behind a couple of parked cars in the far end of the lot. He was backed against a chain-link fence. His options for escape were few.

I questioned my sanity as I eased my way toward him, using the several rows of cars to dodge errant bullets, before finally reaching Spence's side.

"Drake!" Spence was surprised to see me. "What are you doing here?"

"Trying to talk some sense into you."

Spence jumped up and threw a couple of bullets out of his Glock. I heard glass shattering. "Get out of here, man. It's me they want."

"Christ, I know that, but I'm not leaving my new partner high and dry," I shouted as Spence squeezed off a few more shots, emptying his clip. "And quit with the bullets already! You're just playing into their game! Let me talk to the cops for you. We'll let them take you in. These guys are such amateurs, we can have you out of the joint on a technicality in no time."

Spence pulled another clip from his waistband and slammed it into the Glock. He looked at his gun, then me, then the advancing cops, then back to me. Worry filled his eyes.

"Stay put and for God's sake—don't keep shooting at them," I pleaded.

He stared at me, brooding. He held his automatic so tightly it shook in his hand. "Drake, I have something to tell you about these bowling murders, something you need to know."

"You damn well better have something to tell. And I expect you to tell me once I get you out of this mess."

I started off along the fence, hoping my words got through to him. Now all I had to do was figure out how to approach the cops without them shooting me.

I creeped past a row of cars, then turned to check on Spence. All those brains and they didn't stop him from acting stupid in a crisis. He stood up to run toward the diner. Where he thought he would go, I had no idea. I was sure he didn't know either.

"Spence! What are you—" I started to yell at him, but as the shout left my mouth the sound of guns exploded in my ears. I watched helplessly as a bullet ripped through Spence's chest. Some son-of-a-bitch cop had shot him in the back.

He let out a sickening cry and fell forward onto the hood of a car, hitting with a metallic crunch. His gun clattered to the asphalt next to him. He hung on the hood for a moment, then slid slowly to the ground, landing with a heavy thud.

"Damn!" I cursed fate, slamming my pistol into its holster as I ran over to him. I turned him over. He had a hole in his chest. The bullet had gone straight through him, exiting close to his heart. It was bad, one of the worst hits I'd ever seen. There was no doubt about it; Spence wasn't going to live much longer. I slapped my hand over his wound and pressed hard, hoping he would hold on long enough for the ambulance, at the same time knowing he wouldn't.

"Man," he moaned, pain cutting heavily into his voice. "Where's that double-crossing broad?" She wasn't around. He yelled at her anyway. "Thanks for the sour persimmons, bitch."

My mouth rattled off some obscenities of my own as

my mind swam in the thought of Spence's blood. "Hold on . . . just hold on."

I was barely conscious of the booted feet that gathered around us.

Spence's eyes parted slowly and stared at me. "Drake," his voice was all raspy and weak. "I have to tell you," a spasm of coughs racked his body. Blood spurted out of his mouth and flowed freely from his damaged chest.

"What's that?" I asked, pushing down heavily on his injury with my hand, crouching nearer to him.

"Everything . . ." he croaked, ". . . everything is all red herring."

"What?" I shouted at him. "What do you mean by that? Spence? Spence? Answer me, goddamn it!"

There was no answer. Spence Nelson was dead.

Chapter Twenty

BACK SEAT DRIVER

I WAS CRADLING SPENCE'S lifeless body in my arms. His blood soaked into the fabric of my suit, thick and sticky on my arms, chest, and thighs. I remember thinking that my cleaner wasn't going to be very happy with me.

I felt sick. Part of me felt guilty about Spence's death. I'd only known him a short while, but if I ever had a kindred spirit in this business, it was Spence Nelson. I couldn't help but think he'd still be alive if I hadn't been involved. But then he'd be in custody, and prison is no place for a guy like Spence. So maybe he was better off, considering the options.

Another part of me was feeling anxious. I was worried about being caught at the scene. I was supposed to be off this case, and things would get further out of my control if Hal—or Duke Wellington—found out about my being here.

Between the two I was wound tighter than an over-wound alarm clock.

That was when I heard footsteps crunching across the parking lot. The sea of booted feet parted to reveal a pair of beat-up wingtips and a pair of shiny new basketball shoes.

"Well, well, what do we have here?" A voice shocked me out of my thoughts.

I looked up into the face of the short, ape-like man ballooning out of the wingtips. He was all forehead and belly with a wide, flat nose and thinning black hair. He wore brown polyester pants and a cheap dress shirt—open at the neck—under a navy blue TCPD VICE windbreaker. It took a moment for me to realize who he was: Brad Makoff, half of the most notorious vice partnership in Testacy City. The other half, Leo Nolan, was standing right beside him. Nolan was a tall, broad, brown-haired guy in grubby jeans, red polo shirt, and the trademark TCPD VICE jacket. His violent tendencies were legendary among the Testacy City underworld.

These two had made it their personal goal to wipe Testacy City clean of drug dealers, pimps, and pushers. At least that's what they said during press conferences. Fact of the matter is they wanted all that action to themselves. Taking out the competition made things that much easier.

And Spence was competition.

"Hey, Drake!" Makoff demanded. "I asked you what you were doing here."

Never once did I regret upstaging Duke Wellington on the Raspberry Jack case, but every so often it was damn inconvenient to be so easily recognized by cops. It made weaving a good yarn all that much more difficult. Not impossible, though.

Ten or so cops were huddled around Makoff, Nolan, and me. None of them said or did much. If they didn't know my reputation, they certainly knew that of Makoff and Nolan. They were a willing audience to what they probably hoped would be some good entertainment. I tried my best to ignore them.

"Actually, Brad, you asked me what we have here," I corrected, gently lifting Spence's body off my knees and placing it on the pavement. "Well, I don't know what you've got, but I've got one dead informant."

"An' what were you doing, getting information from this scumbag?" Makoff continued with his line of questioning, poking at Spence's motionless body with his foot.

I stood up, brushed off my suit, and began weaving my tale. I started, like all believable fiction, with a solid groundwork of the truth.

"I was working on a case," I looked down at Spence's body again. A pool of blood began to ooze out onto the pavement under him. "He had some information that would've helped me out."

"Yeah? What sort of information?" Makoff asked.

Nolan cracked his knuckles and smiled at me. It wasn't a friendly smile.

"I wish I knew," I shot back. "But your boys killed my man before we got to talk."

"Well, that's just too—" Makoff was interrupted by a commotion from Penny's Lanes.

Three officers were dragging Spence's double-crossing customer out of the building, and they had their hands full. She was an alley-cat, kicking, fighting, biting, scratching, and spitting. It was all these three could do to keep ahold of her, let alone get her under control.

"I did my part!" she screamed, over and over again. "We

had a deal!"

Makoff looked up at Nolan. "Say, Leo, looks like there's a little confusion as to what we promised. Take care of that will ya?"

"Right," Leo nodded and sprinted casually across the parking lot.

When he reached the struggling woman, she calmed down a bit and started to say something to him. She didn't get the chance. He smashed her in the mouth with a ham-sized fist. I saw a few teeth fly out of her head. He followed that up with a left to her temple. She went limp and crumpled to the ground. One of the uniformed cops cuffed her and hauled her off to a flashing squad car. Nolan turned and headed back toward us, dusting off his hands like he'd just finished chopping wood.

"Now what was I sayin'?" Makoff shoved his hands deep in his pockets and smiled. His smile was only slightly friendlier.

"You were asking me about my case," I reminded.

"Right. So how's about it?"

"Look, I don't mind telling you guys anything, but do we need all these uniforms around?"

Nolan got back over to us just in time for Makoff to say to him: "Say, Leo, we need all these blues around like this?"

Nolan took the hint and gestured at the assembled uniforms. "All right, guys, we've got it from here," his big voice boomed with authority.

The ten cops standing around us looked at each other, nodded and murmured to themselves before rapidly dispersing.

"That make you feel better?" Makoff asked, flashing his teeth.

"Yeah, much. Thanks," I returned. "Now what you want to know?"

"Who ya workin' for?"

"I can't tell you that." This client confidentiality bit came in real handy sometimes. If it didn't get me killed first.

Makoff frowned. Nolan went back to cracking his knuckles.

I shifted my strategy slightly. "Okay, let me tell you this. I'm working for a concerned party that wants to stop drugs from getting into Testacy City's high schools."

"And you thought Spence was the source?"

"Well, actually, I was looking for *his* source."

This got them interested.

"And what you find out?" Makoff drilled, almost drooling.

"Before we get into that, let's make a deal," I said with trepidation. I hoped my deal was better than the one Spence's stool pigeon got.

"What ya got in mind?" Makoff squinted his eyes to slits, as if he were trying to see through my game.

"It's like this: I give you Spence's supplier, and you keep me out of your reports."

"That's it?"

"That's it."

The two cops looked at each other, nodded, then turned their attention back to me.

"Deal," Makoff agreed. "Now tell us who you got."

"Okay, here it is: Spence gets, well he used to get, most of his goods from Jack Walker."

"Who's that?" Nolan blurted out. "Some kinda bowler?"

"No! What's wrong with you, man!" Makoff barked. "Jack Walker, the ball bearing guy!" He turned toward me. "You sure about this?"

"Not one hundred percent," I admitted. "I was meeting with Spence tonight to confirm it."

"And you think he'd tell you the truth?"

"Yeah, I do. We had a rapport going, something that took me a long time to establish, something you guys erased with a bullet."

"Well I'll be . . ." Makoff said pensively. "Okay. Give us everything you got, and we'll forget you were here."

It took me another hour to spell it all out for them, how Jack Walker, millionaire industrialist, was up to his eyeballs in drugs. It was hot and juicy gossip, the stuff that made vice cops all quivery inside. And it was all a big, convoluted lie. I figured it was the least I owed my old pal Jack.

Finally, their greed satisfied, they let me go. I wasn't all that sure they'd keep their end of the deal, but I was hoping they'd keep it long enough for me to close this case.

I headed for the Galaxie 500, dog tired. The events of the last few days had left me drained, and I felt as if I were running on fumes. After Spence's death and the subsequent grilling and creative truthing, my brain felt all fuzzy.

I didn't really feel like doing anything but going home

and collapsing. Either that or going back to the Penny's Lanes bar for a couple of stiff drinks. I certainly didn't feel like going home to play with Suzi. But she was waiting for me, and she had information I needed to finish this.

I closed my eyes and once again resisted the urge to go back to the bar. But there could be no turning back now, there could be no rest. Very soon this business was going to come down, and I was going to follow it right to the bottom.

My hand paused a moment on the door handle of my car. I got in and concentrated: Drive home. Get Suzi. Eat. Find out what she knows. Time to relax and sort it all out later.

I started the engine and pulled away from the curb. The cool night air blowing in my open window kept me awake.

I twitched when I suddenly felt the chilly touch of a cold steel barrel against my occipital ridge.

"Oh, come on! I can't believe this!" I said aloud. Somebody big was in my back seat with a gun to my head. I thought garbage like that only happened in the movies.

"Keep driving, cretin." With an accent like that it could only be one person; actually, it could only be one of two persons—Butch or Schultz.

"Ouch, you trying to hurt my feelings? Besides, I'm surprised they taught you 'cretin' in your ESL class." This was one ride that was going to end with a lot of pain. If I didn't start acting tough now, I was dead. I might be dead anyway.

He pressed the barrel tighter against my skull. I continued: "So, you want me to take you anywhere special? Grandma's house?"

"The quarry," he grumbled.

"A party at the quarry? But I forgot all my ball bearings at home. Have any on you?"

"It's no party. Mr. Walker wants to see you in private."

"Say . . . This wouldn't have anything to do with the Biggs murder, would it?"

I was starting to have fun teasing this guy. The fun ended when his left hand wrapped around my throat with a grip that could have ended me right there.

Both my hands instinctively left the steering wheel and tried to break his grip. All I succeeded in doing was making the car swerve all over the road until it skidded to a stop on the shoulder. Thankfully, there was no one else on the road.

He released his hold on me. My head snapped back as I gasped for air. He spoke directly into my ear. "No more talk. Drive."

I did as I was told. We hit the highway and sped out to the old quarry, about forty miles west of the city. I kept quiet all the way.

The night was pitch black as we neared our destination. I had no idea where I was going. Suddenly my hulking passenger told me to turn left. My headlights revealed a small dirt road immediately in front of me. I would have completely missed it had I been driving alone.

I had to slam the wheel hard to make the turn, and the Galaxie fish-tailed across the dust-covered road, tires complaining.

The new road was pretty straight, and up ahead I saw a single white light that could only be our destination. I felt steel prod the back of my skull. I cruised ahead. A rumble from the backseat told me to stop the car underneath the light, which turned out to be a bright floodlight hanging off an old crane. Nice and convenient.

Even with the cone of light coming down from the crane, it was so dark that the moon and the stars cast a blue glow over the landscape.

The lummox in the back dragged me out of the car. Before I could adjust my eyes to the darkness, I could smell the pipe smoke. Then all I remember were fists to my head and body. It wasn't the worst beating I'd gotten in the last few days, but it still took me to my knees.

"Enough." Jack Walker's voice cut through the pain. As much as I hurt, this rich, pompous bastard made me angry enough to forget my hurt.

"Bring me here to kill me, Jack? Like you killed the others?"

"No, Drake. If I wanted you dead, you'd already be dead. No, I brought you here…"

As he paused, I saw his dark silhouette move out from the black toward me.

"I brought you here, Drake, to give you the answers you need."

Chapter Twenty-One

THE RED HERRING SYNDICATE

"ANSWERS? WHAT'S THAT SUPPOSED to mean?" I demanded, crouched on my knees beneath Walker. I didn't like being at his feet like this, but I doubted my ability to stand.

"It means that I've had my eye on you, Drake, from the moment you took this case. If you suspect me of having my hands in more things than the manufacture of ball bearings, you're right—though don't for a moment think that you can pin anything on me."

"Like the Biggs murder?"

"Damn you, Drake, listen for once instead of shooting off your mouth!" He stepped closer into the light, pointing a neatly manicured finger at me. "I'm telling you that I don't have anything to do with either of the dead bowlers!"

"Yeah, okay. You get your goon to drag me out to the middle of nowhere to tell me you're innocent?"

"No. You were dragged out here so I can tell you who the killer is."

I wasn't ready to buy this load of laundry. My insides felt empty, like after having dry heaves. I had nowhere to turn. I pushed: "Are you saying you have a name for me, Jack?"

"Yes, I have a name for you, but it's not exactly what

you're expecting."

"What's that supposed to mean?"

"Just this: Joe Biggs' death wasn't the result of some petty act of vengeance. Rather, it was part of a complex plan designed to muddy the waters, so to speak. More specifically, perhaps, to confuse and confound a certain detective, namely you."

"You're telling me some guy was killed to throw me off of the fact that he was killed? What kind of nonsense—"

"No, no, no, you buffoon. He was killed to throw you off the trail of something bigger than a dead bowler—and I don't mean that literally."

I pushed harder: "Give me the name, Jack."

He lifted one of his legs and knocked out his pipe against the sole of one of his Bruno Maglias. He placed the pipe in the outer breast pocket of his suit. When he was damn well ready, he said: "You're looking for an organization called The Red Herring Syndicate."

Spence Nelson's dying words immediately echoed in my mind. "The Red Herring Syndicate?"

"The Red Herring Syndicate, yes. It's an underground crime organization in Testacy City. Many people are aware of their activity; a small handful have heard the name. Nobody knows anything else. This concerns me only in that this Syndicate continues to ... interfere with some good 'opportunities' that come my way."

"Uh-huh." I felt like an old-style phone operator who'd just had all her plugs pulled from the switchboard; I could almost see the lights flashing as I scrambled to reestablish the connections. "So, how does Suzi Biggs fit into all of this?"

"Hardly at all. I'm done with her. If I can speak frankly, man-to-man, she was an ... *enjoyable* girl to know. And I spent some modest efforts to continue that enjoyment. But enjoyment comes in many colors and many flavors, if you get my meaning, old boy." He let out a deep, lecherous laugh. He tilted his head back, and the flood-light reflected off his eyes.

He looked possessed.

He moved closer to me, but not too close. "So you can have Suzi Biggs. I can be awful generous with my ... hand-me-downs."

My throat burned with rising bile. I funneled all my anger into the energy to stand. If I had been calmer, more relaxed, I would have exploded. But I was beat down enough to be desensitized to his childish instigations. He was pushing my buttons; the only thing I could do was let him and still stand strong.

"Why tell me all this, Jack? Why all of a sudden are you so willing to play ball?"

"I've been playing ball with you from the beginning; you just didn't know the rules of the game. Don't think for a moment that I wouldn't have a troublemaker like you locked away in a jail cell, especially when the police are so eager to do it for me."

If he wanted me to be grateful for his generosity, I wasn't.

"No, I've been testing you, seeing what kind of mettle you have. After you stormed into my office, I knew that if any man could take down the Syndicate, it would be you. You have that kind of fire.

"Don't get the impression, Drake, that I like you. The truth is that I know you're in deep enough, and you're desperate enough, to go out and shake up this group of malefactors. On the one hand, any rabble-rousing that you do to help yourself helps me even more. Of course, on the other hand, whether you choose to ignore me and my gift of information or not, they'll get to you. I'm sure you haven't more than a day—two at the most—to live. Then you won't be bothering me—or anyone for that matter—anymore. Good luck," he sneered.

So I was going to be his tin soldier, wound up and let loose in the minefield.

He was good. I was wound up plenty.

One of the monkeys threw my keys at me. Then all of their figures faded into the deep black surrounding the quarry.

This whole week I'd been collecting pieces of a puzzle that didn't quite fit together. Jack Walker had taken this puzzle and mixed it up good, and suddenly all the pieces were falling right into place. As hazy as my mind was, things were finally starting to make sense to me. I was beginning to see the pattern that spread out over Testacy City.

The more I thought about it as I drove back to town, the more it scared the hell out of me.

The scariest part was that one clue was still missing. Though I had no idea what it was or where to look for it, I knew it was the piece that would bring this whole mess together.

My foot pressed harder on the gas pedal. The city lights

rose in the distance. I remembered the bottle of bourbon I'd left in the car. I grabbed it from under my seat, spun the cap off with my thumb, and poured enough alcohol down my throat to make me cough.

I focused hard on the lights from town. I could imagine the entire city in flames.

That thought kept me company the entire way home.

Chapter Twenty-Two

THE MISSING CLUE

IT WAS A LITTLE AFTER NINE by the time I got home. I was bone-tired, but Walker's information—along with the bourbon I'd sucked down on the ride back to town—had burned away at the fatigue. I could feel that I was close to the end of this.

I opened the door to my apartment and found Suzi Biggs laying claim to my favorite chair. That, I had expected. I had also expected the two of us to hit up a restaurant and get a nice meal, then for me to figure out a way to get the last piece of this puzzle out of her.

What I hadn't expected to see was Henry Goiler standing over her, his 9mm black Beretta stuck in her face.

Last I remember, Goiler was the detective Hal had assigned to the Haufschmidt jewel case. I'd worked with him a couple of times before, and we always had good results, even though his crude ways clashed with mine. Crude or not, he was the last person I expected to be threatening Suzi in my apartment.

His crudeness was all-encompassing. Goiler was a squat little man, pig-like in both appearance and manner. Perched on his head was a brown porkpie hat that was about a size too small. In fact, all of his clothes were too small: his tan pants just brushed the tops of his heavily scuffed brown oxfords, his yellow shirt didn't quite cover the volume of his belly, and his tiny brown necktie—the short, wide kind—looked like it belonged on a teenager. Over the whole ensemble he wore a threadbare brown suitcoat that seemed like it was about to burst its seams.

He looked like a dangerous clown.

"Goiler?!" My voice cracked with confusion. "What are you doing here?"

"Ben!" Suzi cried, panic thick in her voice. "Thank God you're here! This guy burst in here and threatened to kill me!"

I was having a hard time accepting any of this. "Goiler, what's your deal?"

"Like you don't know, Drake," he drawled out of the side of his mouth, not taking his eyes off Suzi.

"I'm not in the mood for this!" The confusion and fatigue only added to my anger.

"Funny, Drake, very funny," Goiler spit out.

The way he spoke required an excess amount of saliva. It wasn't pleasant.

"I don't believe that for a minute. I know the tricks you like to pull, and you can't pull nothin' over on me."

"Come on, Goiler, put the goddamn gun away, and we'll get this straightened out," I pleaded. "Christ, man, you're with the Agency."

"Oh no. The gun stays." He jabbed the Beretta in Suzi's direction. "One false step, and it's curtains for the floozy."

"Hey! I'm no floozy!" Suzi, indignant, started to pull herself up out of the chair.

As she struggled to get up, Goiler backhanded her hard across the face, knocking her solidly back into the chair. "I told you not to move," he emphasized every word with a thrust of his gun.

We weren't going to get to the bottom of this as long as Goiler was waving his gun around. And when he hit Suzi, he'd crossed the line. While he was paying attention to her, I made a play. It turned out to be a lame move. My lunge across the room suffered from bad timing and poor execution. Goiler saw me coming and had plenty of time to move his bulk out of my way. I slid past him, and he clubbed me right behind the ear with the butt of his gun as I went by.

The pain from the blow jarred me all the way to my toes. I lost what little balance I had and tumbled into my television stand, sending its contents skittering across the floor as I continued into the wall on the far side of my cramped living room. I landed with a thump.

"I told you, Drake, no tricks." Goiler walked over to me, snatched my gun from its holster, and put it in his coat pocket. "For safekeepin'." His tiny black eyes glistened like oil-covered BBs from beneath the folds of his puffy face.

When he saw I wasn't moving too fast, he turned his attention back to Suzi. "Now, let's try this again. Where's the bracelet?"

"Ohhh …" Suzi moaned, maybe out of pain, maybe out of frustration.

I pulled myself to a sitting position. "Bracelet?" I rubbed the sore spot behind my ear. It was already starting to swell. "What are you talking about, Goiler?"

"Oh, Ben," Suzi sighed, trying not to look at the gun pointed at her. "This is what I've been trying to tell you this whole time."

"What?" I was getting more confused by the second. "You've been trying to tell me something?"

"Shut up, the both of yous!" Goiler shouted. "I'm not playin' around here!"

"Ben," Suzi started to cry, putting her shaking hands over her flustered face. "I'm so sorry. It's been hard ... so hard ..."

"Awright, stop it with the waterworks, already," Goiler ordered. "I can't stand blubberin' dames."

Suzi sniffed and managed to get herself under control. She looked over at me. "Ben, the day before he died, Joe gave me this diamond bracelet. It was beautiful."

"Aw, for cryin' out loud!" Goiler said. "Enough with the back story. Just fork over the goods!"

I ignored the fat gunman. Now that Suzi was talking, I didn't want her to stop. "A diamond bracelet, huh?"

"It was the nicest thing anyone had ever given me. I mean, people bought me expensive stuff before, but I knew Joe had sacrificed a lot to give me this. We were so happy we went out to have a nice dinner at The Long Mile—"

Goiler broke in: "Nobody cares where you were gonna eat—"

"Come on, man, have some patience. We're not going anywhere," I explained, hoping to cool him off a little. "You've got the gun."

"That's right I got the gun. What I don't got is the damn bracelet!"

Suzi had been holding back with her story for so long,

now that she'd started, it was all flowing out. "The next day Jerry came by. I thought Jerry and I were friends. I thought he was going to comfort me, but instead he demanded that I give him the bracelet," Suzi's tears came back with a vengeance, making it hard for her to speak. "I …played dumb…not wanting to…lose…the last gift Joe …gave…me."

"I can't believe you're telling me this now," I said.

"That's the final camel straw! I've had about enough of all this yammerin'!" Goiler pointed his gun at me. "I want the bracelet. I know she's got it on her, 'cause I already tossed her place and got nothin'."

"Don't listen to him, Ben!"

Goiler turned and belted Suzi alongside her head, knocking her cleanly out of the chair and sending her sprawling on the floor. Still sobbing, she curled up into a little ball.

"I told you to shut up!" Goiler screamed at her, sweat running in torrents down his round forehead.

Seeing Suzi get hit again made me sick to my stomach, but I was too woozy and Goiler was too hopped up for me to try anything. There was nothing I could do except convince her to give him the bracelet.

Silence, except for Suzi's quiet sobbing, filled my apartment.

"I know you got it on you!" Goiler's bloodlust was running hot. His face was a dark crimson, and the veins in his temples throbbed with impatience. "You gonna give it up, or do I gotta strip you?"

"Suzi." I spoke slowly and quietly. I didn't want to say

anything that would set Goiler off worse than he already was.

Suzi opened her eyes and looked at me.

Goiler pulled my gun out of his pocket and started pacing around the room, a gun in each fist, crazy eyes darting between me and Suzi, looking too much like he was deciding who he was going to shoot first.

"I don't care that you haven't told me everything," I told Suzi. "Really I don't. That doesn't matter now. All that matters is getting you out of this safely. So please, if you have the bracelet, give it to him."

"But..." Her eyes pleaded with me.

"Suzi, I know this guy. He's not kidding around. Give him the bracelet."

Suzi pulled herself up into a sitting position. Goiler watched her intently, his big fish-lips twitching, as she slowly unbuttoned the top two buttons of her blouse. She reached under the fabric and dug around in her brassiere. When she pulled her hand back out, she was holding a bracelet made up of the biggest diamonds I'd ever seen. It sparkled brightly in the dim light, and tiny rainbows flashed wildly from its many facets.

It was beautiful.

Suzi held it out to Goiler, eyes cast down at the floor in shame. He dropped my gun back into his pocket and snatched the bracelet from Suzi.

"That's more like it." Smug satisfaction played across his face. "Thanks for your cooperation, Drake."

"Sure, Goiler," I sneered. "Now how about leaving us alone?"

Goiler ogled the bracelet with palpable greed. His big pink tongue flicked out and cleaned the saliva from the corners of his mouth with a heavy slurping noise. He stashed the bracelet in the breast pocket inside his coat.

"Sure, I'll be leavin', all right," he wiped his mouth on the back of his fleshy hand. "But I can't let you stick around to squawk to the cops, so we're all gonna leave together."

"Where ... where ... are we going?" Suzi stammered.

"We're all gonna take a friendly little ride," Goiler's words, full of malice, oozed out from between his spittle-covered lips.

"A ride? Jeez, Goiler. Can you get any more cliché?"

"Shut up, Drake," he threatened. "Let's go." He gestured us to the door with a violent waving of his gun.

With some difficulty, I managed to get my legs under me and walk over to Suzi. She sat on the floor, staring intently at my shattered television.

"Oh, Ben," she wiped tears out of her eyes. "I'm so sorry."

"That's okay, Suzi," I held out my hand, offering to help her up. "Come on. Looks like we're not quite done yet."

She looked up at me and smiled. It was a small smile, but it was genuine.

"I know you'll take care of me, Ben."

She took my hand, and I helped her up.

Her confidence gave me strength.

"Where we going, Goiler?"

"Well, I've got some things to finish tonight, so I thought we'd head out someplace where you two won't be able to cause too much trouble," Goiler said. "I thought we'd head on out to the quarry."

For the second time that night, I drove my car down the desert highway to the quarry at gunpoint. Goiler insisted that he sit in the back where he could easily plug anyone who, in his words, "did anything stupid." That left Suzi sitting next to me, holding tightly to my leg. She was scared. Her long nails dug deeply into the flesh of my thigh.

It wasn't long before Goiler had found my three-quarters empty bottle of Old Grand-Dad rolling around on the floor and started taking heavy pulls from it.

Goiler's reputation as a slob was second only to his reputation as a braggart. I was hoping his pride, in addition to the alcohol he was consuming, would make him open to answering a few questions. I certainly wouldn't have time later when I had to make a move.

"Say, Goiler."

"Yeah?"

"I'm wondering some things," I took a moment to continue, letting curiosity build in my throat. "Now, I've figured out that you were the one who ripped off the Haufschmidt jewels—"

"Did I now?" he interrupted with a coarse laugh.

"And I'm pretty sure you offed Iverson," I continued.

Goiler tipped the bottle to his lips and sucked noisily at the bourbon.

"Yeah," he belched, "well, that's what you call an educated guess there, Drake."

"But I just don't understand why. How's he tied up in

all of this?"

Goiler cackled from the back seat, "And I thought you were a detective."

He took another swig of bourbon.

"Y'see, Iverson wanted to be connected—too many cops-and-robber shows on TV or somethin'.

"Anyhow, I helped him out. He was doing a little free-lance work for me. The guy had the right attitude for crime, but he lacked conviction. And he forgot the first rule I taught him: You don't steal from the big man."

Finding out that Iverson pulled off the Haufschmidt jewel heist with Goiler was one big curveball—and just when I thought I had a handle on this case. That only left one question.

"So did you take out Joe Biggs, too?"

Silence emanated from the back seat. I glanced into my rear-view mirror, but all I saw was the black of the lonely highway. The barrel of Goiler's gun jammed into my head, right behind my ear. Goiler pressed the gun hard against the tender spot where he had clubbed me earlier.

"I think you've asked enough."

He forced the barrel of the gun hard against my bruise. I winced, feeling that shove all through my body. Suzi's nails dug deeper into my leg. I could feel her shaking.

"That's not something you need to know, not where you're goin'," he said. "An' you keep yappin', you're gonna get there faster."

Goiler was just crazy enough to shoot the guy who was driving the car he was riding in. So instead of talking, I started thinking how I could get me and Suzi out of this jam.

My brain needed a little lubricant.

"Okay, then," I resigned. "If you're not going to talk to me, then how about giving me a little of that bourbon?"

More silence, then finally: "Awright, fine. Just don't drink it all," he ordered, handing me the bottle.

He sure hadn't left me much to work with. I took a couple of swallows, getting a good dose of Goiler's spit in the process, and handed it back. The liquor's sweet fire started burning in my throat and rapidly spread to my brain. Now it was time for a plan.

We rode the rest of the way in silence. This ride seemed a lot longer than my last one. Finally, we pulled up under the bright glow of the quarry's floodlight.

"Well, here we are," Goiler announced as I switched off the ignition. "Let's all move real slow, eh?"

We got out of the car and started walking. Goiler was pushing us along from behind, a gun in each fist. He stopped us when we got to the edge of the quarry. We were far enough away from the floodlight so that all I could see in front of me was a yawning pit of black. It was a deep silence.

I turned around, ready to make my play.

The dust we had kicked up shimmered as it settled back to the ground, making me feel like I'd slipped into a dream. The distant light behind Goiler streamed around him, cutting a man-shaped hole into the dust. The silhouette was as dark as the void behind me.

His mood seemed positively lighter, and he chuckled with glee as he said:

"Okay, Drake. You got any last requests?"

Chapter Twenty-Three

LENINGRAD RULES

"YOU KILL MANY PEOPLE out here, Goiler?" I asked, trying to sound casual.

"What sort of trick are you tryin' to pull?"

He looked at me quizzically.

"None at all. I'm just wondering how often you bring people out here and shoot 'em."

"A couple of times, I guess."

"Huh. You kill many people?"

"Ben…" Suzi whined, confused about what was running through my head. I couldn't blame her, I wasn't so sure myself.

"What's with all the questions?" Goiler barked.

"I'm just curious, so I thought I'd take you up on that last-request offer and ask a few."

He glared at me and wiped the sweat from his ample forehead.

"Yeah, I've killed a few folks, sure. Okay?"

"Doesn't it get boring after a while?" I let loose with a little chuckle. "I read that somewhere."

"What do you mean?"

"I would guess it gets boring, all that death. You've got to keep coming up with more and more interesting ways to kill people to keep it fun, right?"

"I guess so…" He was still trying to figure out what I was

up to. I was hoping I could keep him guessing until he was too caught up in my scheme to quit.

"What's the most interesting way you've ever killed someone?"

He thought a moment before he said: "I guess once when I gave this guy a Colombian neck tie—"

"That's your most interesting murder?" I interrupted. "That's pretty boring, Henry."

"What . . . what do you mean?" I was starting to rattle him.

"Goiler, your problem is you've got no style."

"Style?"

"Yeah, style. I'll bet you're always in a rush and miss the finer points."

"Heh," he said, switching to the defensive. "Well, I get the job done."

"Sure you do," I agreed, "like Jerry Iverson."

"Yeah, like him. I already told you that," he snapped, his irritation at my questions building.

"Yeah, but you messed up, didn't you."

"Whaddya mean? He's dead, ain't he?"

"Yeah, but it was supposed to look like a suicide, wasn't it?"

"Yeah . . ."

"And it didn't. You screwed up."

Silence.

I turned it up a notch: "I bet the Red Herring Syndicate wasn't happy about that, were they?"

"What are you talking about?" Goiler exploded. "I'm part of the Red Herring Syndicate!"

"How long have you been working for them?"

"*With* them," he corrected. "I've been working *with* them for a long time. Years."

"And you're still a pawn to them, just a little man to be shoved around. Dirty work needs doing? No problem, call Henry Goiler: 'Henry, do this. Henry, do that. Henry, kill Jerry Iverson. And don't mess it up this time!' But you did."

"Why you…"

"And you know why? 'Cause you're a screw-up with no style."

"You want style?" Goiler screamed at me. Even in the darkness I could see his puffy face turn bright red with anger. "You want style? I'll kill *you* with style!"

He leveled his gun at my head. He was so mad he couldn't hold it steady.

"How? Shoot me in the head and leave my body in the desert?" I snarled: "That's not style."

"You got a better idea?"

"As a matter of fact I do." My throat was parched. I ran my dry tongue across my lips. "Are you a gambling man?"

"Sure," his eyes squinted with confusion. "I like to play the ponies."

"That's good, cause I'd like to challenge you to a game. Just me and you."

"A game?"

He took a wary step backward, gun still pointed at my head.

"Yeah, a simple game," I was feeling the adrenaline pump through my veins, knowing I was putting it all on the line. "If you win, you can do whatever you have to do with no interference from me."

"Oh, and let me guess," Goiler laughed, "if you win I gotta let you go?"

"Me and Suzi. Exactly." I waited for Goiler to respond. He didn't, so I prodded him along: "So, you up for it?"

"Maybe," Goiler scratched the side of his face with the barrel of his gun. "Depends what game we're playin'."

I paused, letting the silence of the night sink in before I responded with:

"Russian Roulette."

"Oh God, no, Ben!" Suzi cried. She fell down at my feet, looking up at me, pleading.

Russian Roulette was an absurd and dangerous idea, but Goiler was an absurd and dangerous man. I needed this distraction so I could catch him off guard just long enough to get the upper hand.

"Jesus!" Goiler exploded. "I've known you to do some crazy things, Drake, but…but… You're out of your damn mind!"

"Scared, Henry?" I asked, whispering.

"Shut up!"

"It's okay if you are; it takes a real man to play Russian Roulette."

"I said shut up!" Goiler looked down at the gun he held in each hand, thought creasing his brow.

"I ain't afraid, Drake. Not of you. And not of some silly game of yours."

He broke my gun open, carefully keeping the Beretta trained on me. With his thumb he held in one round as he tipped the gun back allowing the remaining four rounds to fall to the dusty ground. He snapped it shut with a flick of his wrist and gave the cylinder a hefty spin.

He handed the gun to me, barrel first.

"Okay. Let's do it. You first," he rumbled, aiming the barrel of the Beretta directly at my face, just below my left eye. "And if you don't pull that trigger, I'll do it for ya."

I was gambling with my life, and that didn't bother me. What did bother me was the fact that I was gambling with Suzi's life, too. But despite that, I had to forge ahead. This was the only chance she had.

I could see Goiler trembling; I couldn't tell if it was out of excitement or out of fear.

My thoughts flashed back to the day—was it only yesterday?—that I stormed into Jack Walker's office. That was a pretty risky move then, but I got out of it just fine. Maybe I'd get out of this jam in one piece, too. I just had to stay one step ahead of Goiler.

"Wait," I said, looking into Goiler's bloodshot eyes.

Suzi's crying lessened to a soft whimper before she held her breath, waiting for Goiler to respond. The absence of her sobbing left a tension that was terrifying.

"Scared, Drake?" Goiler asked.

"No, I just need to know which rules we're playing by."

"Whaddaya mean, rules?"

"There's two different versions of the game," I explained, "St. Petersburg rules and Leningrad rules."

"What the hell's the difference?"

"In St. Petersburg rules you spin the cylinder between every pull of the trigger, but in the original version,

Leningrad rules, you spin it only after everyone playing has had a turn."

"I don't care," Goiler said. "Whatever you want, let's just get this over with. No, wait. Let's play Leningrad rules. That sounds more fun."

"Fine, then."

"Yeah, fine. Now quit stallin' and play!" Goiler ordered, prodding me with the Beretta.

As my finger tightened on the trigger, visions of my wife, alive, vibrant, and beautiful played in my head. The roar of blood between my ears was deafening. I focused on the images of my wife ... squeezed ... and ...

Click.

Goiler took the gun out of my numb hand and started laughing.

"Damn, Drake! I didn't think you had the stones to do it!"

"Your turn, Henry," I deadpanned. "Do you have the stones?"

Goiler suddenly stopped laughing. "Damn right I do. But first ..."

He held the gun out to Suzi.

"No ... oh no ..." Suzi whined, her face wet with tears. She held her hands defensively outward and frantically waved them about like she was trying to escape a cloud of insects. She backed away from Goiler as he approached her with the gun.

"Goiler, leave Suzi out of this," I warned. "This is just you and me playing."

"I'm in charge here, Drake," Goiler's laugh took on a

more maniacal quality. "An' I say she plays."

There wasn't much I could do, not while he held that Beretta on Suzi. I knew if I made a move, he'd kill her.

Suzi took the Smith & Wesson from Goiler and sank to her knees.

"Please, no," she begged, looking for mercy in Goiler's cold eyes, her arms held limply at her side. Then she looked at me. The tears on her cheeks glistened in the dim light, and her big eyes were glazed over with fear.

"Ben … Ben … I don't want to die."

"Yeah, yeah," Goiler aimed the Beretta at her forehead, careful to not turn his back to me. "Just get on with it."

Suzi lifted the gun to her left temple, barely having the strength to hold it there. Her whimpering echoed out across the quarry and got deep in my ears, bringing a guilt, thick and heavy, that settled in the pit of my stomach.

"Come on, Goiler," I pleaded, "leave her out of it."

Goiler looked back over his shoulder and shouted: "Drake, she's playin'. You quit complainin' about it, or I'll finish her right here!" His voice was rich with hostility.

"Please …" Suzi whined.

"Pull the trigger, or I shoot you right now," Goiler growled.

I stood there, feeling powerless as each of Suzi's sobs brought more pain to the sickness in my stomach.

After an eternity of waiting, I heard a loud click. Suzi collapsed in a heap on the ground, her body twitching in spasms. She cried for all she was worth. Poor kid. I had to end this soon.

Goiler stood over her laughing uproariously. "That was

great! You should have seen her eyes, Drake. Just like a deer caught in the headlights!"

"Okay, Goiler, your turn."

"Actually," he handed the gun to me, "I think it's your turn. That was just a warm-up round."

"That's not playing by the rules, Henry."

"I decided we're playing 'Goiler's rules'," he answered. "And that means it's your turn."

I figured Goiler was gambling on one of us getting killed before he even had to play. While that may have been his plan, it sure wasn't mine. I promised myself I'd do this one more time, then I'd make my move. But if he wasn't going to play by the rules, I wasn't either. And I needed better odds. I spun the cylinder.

"Hey, what gives? Who said you could spin?" Goiler squealed.

I chose not to answer. I put the gun to my head, closed my eyes, and squeezed the trigger. It was easier the second time.

A long keening wail erupted from Suzi Biggs that seemed to go on forever. It sounded like someone was dragging a serrated blade across her belly.

I handed the gun back to Goiler.

"Are you going this time Goiler? Or are you afraid to take your turn again?"

"I'm not afraid! I'll show you!"

This was the moment I'd been hoping for—I'd jump Goiler during that second of hesitation when, holding a gun to his own head, he contemplated the consequences of pulling the trigger.

Goiler grabbed the Smith & Wesson from me, spun the cylinder, brought it to his head, and squeezed the trigger. All in one fluid motion.

Click.

There went my chance. Just like that.

"There, Drake!" Goiler tittered. "You happy?!"

"Yeah, couldn't be happier."

This bad idea just got worse. A lot worse.

He turned to Suzi, still lying in a heap in the dirt, and held the gun out to her.

"Your turn again, doll."

Suzi broke down into hysterics, hyperventilating uncontrollably.

"No, not again. I can't do it again. Don't make me. Don't make me. Please."

"You can thank your new boyfriend, Ben Drake, for this world of pain. This is his game. You're gonna play 'cause that's what he wants," the twisted words slithered out of Goiler's throat. "Now play!"

Suzi gingerly took the gun and held it to her head for a moment, then let her arm fall to the ground.

"Wait! I can't go ... I just remembered ... my puppies are at home ... and there's nobody to feed them. I can't do this! I can't die! Who's going to take care of Laza and Apsos? Who'll care for my little puppies?"

"Come on, woman, we ain't got all night!" Goiler pulled back the hammer of his Beretta. "Play the game!"

Again Suzi placed the gun against her temple.

A cold chill ran down my spine. I had a bad feeling about this. I lunged at Goiler and yelled:

"Suzi don't!"

Goiler saw me coming and spun to meet me, firing the Beretta in the process. The shot went wide, echoing off the quarry walls. I was close enough to the gun that it set off a ringing in my ears. The night suddenly seemed wrapped in cotton.

I tackled Goiler, taking him to the ground.

We struggled, rolling dangerously close to the edge of the quarry. Goiler grunted and flailed his legs. I pinned his gun arm beneath my knee.

Inexplicably, Goiler kept on squeezing the trigger, sending bullets off into space. He was too busy trying to keep hold of his gun to do any sort of real fighting. One by one I pried his thick, strong fingers from the pistol.

I got the Beretta out of his grasp. Now I had to put him down quick.

I hauled off and belted him across the jaw with the butt of the gun. I was rewarded with a loud crack as the bone broke beneath my blow.

Goiler howled like a wounded dog and clutched his jaw with both hands. He rolled back and forth, as if that would ease his pain.

I figured that would occupy him for a while, so I bolted over to Suzi's side. She was lying on the cold ground, motionless. When I reached her I saw why.

Her blank eyes stared vacantly at me. Her mouth hung slightly open. The whites of her eyes and her pearly teeth glowed eerily in the pale, dim light.

A small, charred wound marred the left side of her head. A larger, bloodier wound blew out the opposite side of her skull. A thick trickle of viscous liquid, a mingling of blood and brains, oozed from the gaping hole.

I felt like someone had turned me inside out. The sickness in my stomach rose to my mouth and sent the contents of my guts spewing out hotly onto the desert ground. I wiped my mouth on the back of my hand and watched the sand absorb my steaming bile.

I heard a scraping sound behind me, so I spun around in time to see Henry Goiler struggling to get up. He was making a strange "wuffling" noise. It took me a moment to realize that it was the sound of a man with a broken jaw trying to laugh hysterically.

My vision turned red. For a moment I hated Henry Goiler with every fiber of my being. He was a despicable wretch who deserved to die.

I shot him twice in the head with his own gun. He fell backward and landed with a sickening thump. I fell, first to my knees then to my back. All the strength was gone from my body. It was the first time I'd deliberately killed anyone. The first time I'd committed murder.

The events of the night played again and again in my head. I kept changing things slightly hoping for a better outcome, but it always ended with Suzi's death.

I don't know how long I stayed like that, lying on the ground, looking up at the stars.

When I got up, I retrieved my empty gun from where it had landed beside Suzi. I went over to Goiler and pulled the diamond bracelet out of his pocket. I kicked his lifeless body over the quarry and stood there until I could no longer hear it sliding down the steep embankment. I tossed his gun after him.

I kept looking back over my shoulder as I trudged to my car, hoping that Suzi would get up and be all right, knowing it was a ridiculous fantasy.

Chapter Twenty-Four

TELL ME TOMORROW

NOTHING COULD POSSIBLY SHAKE the image of Suzi Biggs from my mind. So on the hard, lonely drive back to my apartment, I thought of nothing.

At night the desert was cold. I drove with the window down. The air that rushed into my car made the sound of a low dirge. My teeth were clenched shut, and I grasped onto the steering wheel like it was the neck of my worst enemy.

I'm not a man who takes to crying; nevertheless, I wiped my eyes, knowing that the tears were in there somewhere and that they were bound to come out sooner or later.

When I got home, the door was unlocked. I pushed it open and entered the darkness with resigned indifference. If someone was waiting to ambush me, I would put up no fight. But I knew there would be no one there.

I walked into my kitchen and instinctively opened the refrigerator. I wasn't even slightly hungry, which was good because it held nothing but condiments, sour milk, and leftovers that should have been thrown out long ago. I was barely awake enough to stand. I just wanted desperately to keep moving, away from today and tonight, into tomorrow.

Tomorrow this case would be over. I knew that.

I closed the refrigerator door and looked around aim-lessly. I saw the paper coffee cup that Suzi had brought with her this morning. Christ, how could that have been this morning? I thought about her slapping me and her saying I wasn't a hero. I thought about us spending the day together at the animal park, acting like kids on a date. I slammed my fist on the counter.

"This isn't fair," I said aloud, simply to hear myself say it.

I had this sudden urge to be instantly unconscious. I headed straight for bed, not even pausing to turn the lights out. I collapsed face down on the mattress. As I dug my head into the pillow I could smell her perfume—a faint scent remaining from when she had cried there this morning.

I should have slept in my chair, I thought. Too late now; I wasn't in any condition to move a muscle. I was out cold in seconds.

Morning came, and I just let it carry on. I felt no more desire to move than I had last night. However, now that my eyes were open, I couldn't get back to sleep.

The phone rang. I didn't answer it. Some time later, it rang some more. I still didn't answer it.

But it got me thinking. I had a plan for how this whole mess would get wrapped up. The first thing I had to do was set that plan in motion. That involved some phone calls.

I dragged myself out of the bedroom and made the three calls I needed to make. They weren't easy. I had to pretend I was more in control of the situation than I really

was; certainly, I couldn't let anyone know what had happened last night. Not yet. Despite my inner uneasiness, the calls came off okay.

I jumped into a long shower. The only other thing I had to do before tonight was stop in the office. I didn't want to have to come back here after that. So after I was cleaned up and dressed real nice, I did one final check to make sure I had everything I needed. The last thing I did was clean my gun. Spinning the cylinder to check that it was oiled right sent chills up my spine.

Rhoda Chang stood up when I came through the door. Her eyes went big as she glanced toward Hal's office and then back at me. She exaggerated her frown so that I could see her tiny teeth.

"I take it the boss ain't too happy?" It was mostly rhetorical; if everything had been hunky-dory I wouldn't have bothered to stop in.

With downcast eyes she shook her head no.

"I don't suppose he found out that I was at the bowling alley yesterday?"

Slowly and with sympathy she nodded her head yes.

"Thanks for the warning, Rhoda."

I managed to break my stoic expression long enough to wink at her. Damn cops. When I made the deal with Makoff and Nolan to keep me out of their report, I didn't really expect them to play fair. I was just hoping to buy some time. Looks like all I bought was a fast train ticket to an earful of heat.

When I entered Hal Reddy's office, the hell I'd expected

launched out of his mouth like a rocket to the morgue. All I could make out between the spittle and swear words was Hal's distinct brand of frustrated anger.

"I'm not going to argue with any of your accusations, Hal. Right or wrong, I had my reasons; now I got to see it play out."

Hal was flicking his ear, the one with the piece missing out of it. I'd seen him do this at other times when he was frustrated and wanted to remind people—and probably himself as well—that he could take a lot and still not back down.

Hal turned down the volume of his voice, which meant he turned up the sarcasm. "I suppose you're so wrapped up in right and wrong that ya forgot ya got a boss to answer to?"

"I know this isn't going to make you happy, but I've been working straight for the mother. And I know this means I might lose my job, but I can't let the lady down. Besides, I know who the killer is."

"You know better than to play games with me. If ya got a name then let's hear it."

"All I ask is that you believe I've got a plan that will put all the problems churned up by this murder to rest. I'm meeting with the killer at the bowling alley bar tonight. If you're going to fire me, tell me tomorrow. Tonight, I have work to do."

As I turned to go, I expected more screaming, maybe even something thrown at me. Instead, Hal Reddy just sat there fuming, his finger flicking his one ear.

It was all about waiting now. A large chunk of the day was already gone, and I wanted to spend the rest of it alone. I don't remember exactly where I went. Where I went and what I did are not important.

What's important is that I walked down a dusty street into the open arms of Testacy City and became one of her ghosts.

Chapter Twenty-Five

DRINKS WITH THE KILLER

I WALKED INTO PENNY'S LANES Bowling Center for what I knew would be the last time. For all the hours I had recently spent here, everything felt new. I was immediately overwhelmed by the low rumble of rolling balls and the crash of falling pins. I was aware of the twangy country-western music that played in the background.

And I noticed that lane thirteen was back in operation; the young family gathered there was bowling happily, oblivious to the murder that had happened where now they stood.

I walked slowly to the bar, right past Enrico, the shoe-shine boy. He called out to me, "Shine, Mister?" I turned away, surprised that he didn't seem to recognize me. Maybe he did, because he kept after me: "Come on, Mister, how's about a shine? They're some nice shoes you got. I could shine 'em up real good!"

I disappeared into the comfort of the bar. It was empty.

After my first glass of bourbon, I had the feeling that the killer might be stalling, hoping that I'd drink myself out of commission before he got here. When Mabel came back to get me another glass, I switched to ginger ale I wanted to keep a clear head, and without a steady flow of drinks to soothe my raw nerves, my small cigars had to carry that burden. Waiting was always easier with tobacco.

I kept my back to the door of the bar. I didn't want to seem too anxious. I knew the killer would show up at some point.

Shortly after midnight, after several hours of waiting, I heard a body shuffle up behind me. The foul-smelling smoke of a cheap dimestore cigar told me my hunch was right. I glanced to my right and saw Hal Reddy sit down on the barstool next to me. I said, "I wasn't one hundred percent sure it was you until now. Here." I pulled out the diamond bracelet and slid it across the bar counter toward him.

"What's this?" he asked, nonplussed.

"The missing Haufschmidt jewel, of course. I figure you were in on that, too."

"You keep working on all the cases I kick ya off of?"

"Don't play dumb, Hal. Time for that is over."

"What kind of fool ideas you got cooking in that noodle of yours, Drake?"

"Goddamn it, Hal!" I said in a loud whisper, not wanting to start a commotion. "I'm trying to level with you. Now you level with me. Here's how I figure all this played out:

"You, Hal Reddy, are the head of the Red Herring Syndicate. Something must have got to you in L.A. back when you worked homicide. When you moved up here, the town was ripe for someone to take it over. So you got this bright idea: start a detective agency and gather as much information about the crime world as you could. Once you got set up and established a reputation and all, you brought on a select group of people you knew you could really trust—people who were in this for the long haul and not out to make a quick black buck. They do all the 'administrating,' so most people in the Syndicate, the people under them who do the dirty work, don't know who the real boss is.

"Even better is the fact that you can set up crimes and then put your own detectives on the cases to 'solve' them—the driving force behind the Red Herring Syndicate being to pull off random, almost absurd crimes that you can frame on some hapless pigeon. That way, the media's attention turns away from the big money capers.

"This case is the perfect example. You found out that an enormous collection of jewels was coming into the city. You and your inside buddy Henry Goiler staged a heist. Though, let me tell you, Goiler wasn't the man you thought he was. But I'll get to him soon enough. Then all you had to find was a punk who was expendable in case you needed a fall guy. Enter young wanna-be crook, Jerry Iverson.

"After the robbery, Mrs. Haufschmidt came to the Always Reddy Agency. This was nice and convenient for you because she brought with her a list of the stolen jewelry. That's when you found out a bracelet was missing.

"Of course, Iverson is the main suspect; his first job and already he's trying to skim off the top. You get Goiler to brace him with the question, and he finds out that bone-head Jerry gave the rocks to his bowling buddy, Joe Biggs, so that Joe could keep his marriage from slipping away.

"So you had to come up with a new plan: kill Gentle-man Joe with an over-the-top display of violence to take the spotlight away from the stolen jewels. The public would become obsessed with finding out who could commit such an atrocity, which means the police would feel the pressure to find the killer quickly. Then a couple days later you have Iverson killed, making it look like he hanged himself. There'd be enough circumstantial evidence to connect him to the Biggs murder, so the police would have a nice, neat package to sell to the news hounds. By that time, the jewel heist would be yesterday's news.

"Didn't count on me being smart enough to figure all this out, did you, Hal? You thought I'd be just as gullible as the police on this one. What you really didn't count on was Jerry Iverson talking to me about Suzi Biggs' affair with Jack Walker."

"What?" Hal blurted out. It was delivered with just enough surprise to make me believe that he really didn't know about it. That was good; telling him something he didn't know would give me a small advantage.

"Getting beat up by Walker's goons—that's not my idea of a good time, Hal. I'd love to knock him down a few notches. That's why we're here. I have a proposition for the leader of the Red Herring Syndicate. I was pretty sure that was you, but I had to get you to meet me here to be certain. Well, here you are, so let me give you my offer."

I paused. He eyed me suspiciously.

"I want in. Cut me a piece of the action."

"You're mad in the head, boy."

Hal waved the old bartender over his way and ordered

a bottle of light beer.

"No way, my head's crystal clear now. I've come this far. I figured you out. Now deal me in. I've shown good faith here, returning the bracelet to you. Oh yeah, I forgot to tell you about your man Goiler. I saw Goiler tonight, and he sold you out."

"What do you mean he sold me out?"

"You heard me. He filled me in on most of the details I was missing. If you don't believe me, take a trip to the quarry, maybe his corpse'll tell you something."

"His corpse?"

"That's right. I shot him and dumped the body. He was afraid of you, afraid of what you'd do to him if he couldn't get the bracelet. That's when I saw my opportunity: I put the plug in him, drove over to Suzi Biggs' place and got her to show me the bracelet. Then I put a plug in her. I'll tell Mother Biggs that Suzi had something to do with her husband's murder, and that she's fled the city. No one's going to miss her."

I wondered if Hal was going to bite. He said, "You killed Suzi Biggs?"

"That's right."

He twitched in his seat. His eyes stayed on me even as he tilted his head back to take long swallows of his light beer. He drank like a college boy. I got the impression he was trying to figure me out, and that had him on the defensive. Right where I wanted him.

I stood up. "Maybe you don't understand me, Mr. Reddy, but I've got you, got you right where I want you."

He chuckled at this.

"All right, laugh if you want to. What you have to understand is I'm not backing down. This city has Benjamin Drake's name all over it, and I'm taking hold of it. You don't want to deal me in, I'll go right through you. I bet Jack Walker would be interested in finding out the name behind the Red Herring Syndicate."

"You can't take me down." Hal pointed a finger at me. He was talking between gritted teeth.

"I can and I will, you smug bastard. That is, unless you're ready to play ball with me. Actually, forget it. I've given you chance enough; I'm going to see my new buddy, Jack."

"You little worm—I'll step on you and smear your guts on the cement."

"Why, Hal? Why did you kill Gentleman Joe Biggs?"

His eyes lit up like a maniac's. I went too far with that last line.

"Ya trying to get a confession out of me? Cops got ya all wired up? Well, you're not going to get me to confess to anything."

The fire in his eyes flickered. He pulled a huge Colt Python from his jacket. He leveled the gun at me inconspicuously enough, but it was hard to be too subtle with a piece like that.

"Come on, Ben, let's go back to the office. I've got another case for you."

I leaned back against the bar. "Maybe you haven't been listening. I don't work for you any more. Now that I figured out how you operate, I'll be calling the shots. Me and Mr. Walker, that is."

Hal's temper was getting the best of him. He lunged at me, throwing his empty left fist at my head.

I was prepared for this, and even though Hal's swing came at me fast, I managed to duck under his roundhouse, balling my hands into fists. I shot back up, bringing with me five hard knuckles to Hal's chin. Despite this solid punch, he was already sending a left jab to my forehead. It connected with a heavy thump. I stumbled back and fell to the floor.

His blow left me woozy. Before I could shake it off, he was on top of me—the gun at my temple and his meaty, heavy hand around my throat.

My hands shot immediately to my neck and tried to loosen the grip his strong fingers had on me.

Mabel spoke up sternly: "You boys want to have a rumble, then take it outside. This is a *family* establishment. Don't make me call the cops!"

I could see the sweat start to bead on Hal's bald head at the mention of the word "cops."

His hand still around my neck, he slammed my head to the floor. It didn't help my wooziness, but at least I was still conscious. He should've known I have a hard head.

He got up, hid his gun, and moved to the wide exitway of the bar. As I struggled off the floor, I saw him turn to the left, then waffle nervously and go the other way. So he was rattled and in flight. Good.

When I scooted out of the bar, I did a quick eyeball of the scene; I saw what spooked him: some boys in blue were loitering to the left near the entrance. Unfortunately for Hal, there was no exit in the direction he headed.

Hal knew the layout of this place; after all, he was here a week ago. There were two walkways on either end of the lanes that led into the back of the building. But as I knew from Dino's brief tour, the exit back there was on the left as well. Doing his best to look casual, Hal hurried down the right walkway, through the narrow door.

I didn't have time to be discreet, because I knew that once he got into the back he would bolt for the exit. So I sprinted across the lanes, jumping the gutters, side-stepping oncoming balls. Some bowlers shouted out rude names at me. Rude names I could handle. At least they weren't carrying guns.

As I went through the door Hal had used, I pulled out my Small Frame Model 637. I let it lead the way around the bulk of the monstrous pinsetting machines. Hal was running down the narrow back corridor.

"Stop running, Hal! It's all over."

He turned to face me, his gun zeroed on my chest, mine on his. His chin was raised in the air as he tilted his head side to side like a snake about to strike. He walked slowly toward me, his eyes drilling into mine.

"Shoulda let me walk out of here, Ben. Now I gotta put you down."

"You'll go down with me. That how you want this to end?"

He continued to pace slowly toward me. "If ya want to end it here, I'll end it here."

My gun arm felt stiff and heavy, but I kept my piece pointed at him. The closer he got, the more certain it was that we both wouldn't miss.

"Christ, Hal, you're a psychopath, you know that? You're a grade-A, certified nut-case. It *was* you that killed Gentleman Joe. You did it with your own crazy-man hands."

He got closer still. He shouted over the roar of the machinery: "And do you know why? He had integrity and conviction. He really loved that slut wife of his. He would have rather died than disappoint her." He cursed. "If I could smash those bowling balls against his happy little head one more time I would!"

I'd had enough. I said, "Stop right there, Hal! Drop the damn gun, or I drop you!"

He fired his gun.

My gun went flying from my hand as I staggered backward into the wall. My legs went out from under me, and I went down. I didn't dare take my eyes off Hal to look at my wound, but I knew from the pain that he'd clipped my right shoulder.

He came closer and towered over me, gun in my face. He said, "Well, Ben, it's been a pleasure working with you. But I'm afraid I have to let you go."

The back doors flew open with a metallic clang. "Freeze, sucker!" It was Duke Wellington and Weisnecki, finally come to join us.

Hal turned and fired on them. That gave him just the moment he needed to climb up into the machines. He reached the overhead catwalk and crouched there, using one of the support beams for cover.

He had nowhere to go, and I think he knew it. He stood up to shoot off a couple rounds at them, but all he did was open himself up. One of the cops' shots connected, and blood spouted from Hal's neck. He let loose a gargled cry of pain and fell back into the huge machine's inner workings.

I looked over at my shoulder. To my surprise, Hal had only grazed me. But it was enough to get blood all down my sleeve and for it to hurt like hell.

I scuffled over to where Hal lay. His body was mangled, twisted wildly between the metal bars and wheels of the pinsetting machine. A wicked-looking piece of metal had pierced through his belly. His eyes were twitching and he was losing a lot of blood. Duke Wellington strolled over, slid his big gun into its holster, and looked down at Hal.

As if Hal could sense us there, he managed, gritting his teeth against the pain, to lift his head and focus his eyes on me.

"Damn you, Drake," he croaked. "You weren't supposed to figure this out. No one was." He coughed violently, spitting a mouthful of foamy blood all over the front of his shirt. "I should have given this case to Manetti."

His head fell back against a metal bar with a sickening thud, but he managed to keep his eyes fixed on me.

Duke Wellington and I just stood there and watched the life fade out of Hal's eyes. His wounds were far too severe for us to do anything else. Then in my mind, one last problem jumped out at me. Not so much a problem as it was an anomaly. I had to say, "Wait a second! If you didn't know about Jack Walker and Suzi Biggs, why did you plant ball bearings at both crime scenes?"

Hal gasped for air. I could barely make out his last words: "What ball bearings?" Then he closed his eyes, and his body was still. Maybe I imagined it, but the faint trace of a smile seemed to flicker across his face.

"Well, Drake," Duke Wellington drawled, "looks like you were right . . . again." I thought I heard the tiniest bit of admiration slipping out from behind the gruffness in his voice.

One of the three calls I'd made that morning was to Duke Wellington. When I laid out the whole scenario for him, he was skeptical. But despite his feelings toward me, he knew that I was good at solving convoluted cases, and he knew me well enough to know that I wouldn't be setting my boss up for a hard fall if I didn't have a damn good reason.

"So, are we finished here, then?" I asked.

He nodded his big head. "Yeah, we're finished. I think we've got everything we need. Don't go skipping town on us, though," he ordered. "Just in case we don't."

"Don't worry, I'm not going anywhere."

"Yeah? So now whatcha gonna do, hotshot?"

"First, I'm going to sleep for a few days. Then, it looks like I'm in business for myself."

"Jesus!" Duke Wellington spouted. "That's all this town needs is a goddamn lone-wolf Ben Drake runnin' around stickin' his nose in all the places it don't belong!"

I couldn't let him have the last line. "Come on, DW, you

didn't think I'd want to stop solving your cases just because my boss is dead?"

He had more to say, but I wasn't hearing any of it. I walked outside and took a breath of late night air.

I'd made two other calls this morning. One was to Elizabeth Biggs, letting her know that this mess was about to come to an end. She told me over and over how proud she was of me and that she knew I was the right man for the job.

Without going into detail I told her that I knew of two little dogs that suddenly found themselves without a home. I figured they'd be good company for her. She seemed to agree, even though this made her start in with the questions. I promised I'd give her the whole story later. We made plans to have coffee together next week.

As usual, talking to her made me feel good. Her words gave me the strength to see the night's events through to the bloody end.

As I walked to my car, I realized I was shaking, the reality of the evening finally overriding the blur that comes with a rush of adrenaline. I paused, lit a cigar, and continued across the parking lot.

I was glad—and more than a little surprised—to find Rebecca Hortzbach leaning against my powder-blue Galaxie 500, smoldering cigarette between her lips. My third call had been to her, and I hadn't expected to see her until later this week. It'd been a long time since I'd seen her in street clothes. It didn't take me long to notice she looked great.

Rebecca took a long last draw on her cigarette, then

flicked the butt across the dark lot. "Looks like you need to relax. Let's take care of that shoulder and get you some breakfast."

I tugged on the knot of my tie and unbuttoned my collar. "Sure. You got any ideas on where to go?"

"Ben, my dear, I've got plenty of ideas."

"Yeah, that's what I was hoping you'd say."

THE END

ACKNOWLEDGEMENTS

We found it impossible to write about a murder in a bowling center without some sound counsel from bowling professionals. To the rescue came Dick Moore of The Bowler's Supply in Burbank, who provided us with valuable information on the technical and stylistic aspects of bowling, and Clay of Hollywood Star Lanes and Raymond and Mouse of Santa Monica's Bayshore Bowl (which incidentally features the coolest bowling alley bar that we've ever been in), who gave us the scoop on the inner workings of the bowling center.

We are grateful to Adam Waldman for lending his graphic design talents to making the cover come alive. Likewise, a round of applause goes to Lisa Palmer and Chris Payne for their valuable advice about the cover's color scheme.

Thanks to all the people who supported *By the Balls* by reading the daily serial featured on the Internet. Specific thanks to Mike Dale, Stevie Sackin, Robert Chamberlain, Joe Barker, Diana Atkinson, Barbara Burlington, and Jonell Napper (of www.hellboy.com), all of whom not only read it regularly, but also provided us their feedback and encouragement along the way.

There have been many others who have supported us from the onset of this project, specifically, Gaston Dominiguez of Meltdown, David Firks of *Blue Murder* (www.bluemurder.com), Molly Lavik of The Larkin Group, Larry Young of PlaNetLar, Rory Root of Comic Relief (who illustrated how to properly conduct a raffle), and Carrie Benton (who selflessly gave her time and valuable public relations experience).

A tip of the fedora to Ed Uthman, whose vivid description of an autopsy refreshed memories of high school field trips to the morgue and college physiology classes.

A few people in the UglyTown pantheon get recognition for simply being: Mark Yturralde, man among men; Simon Leake at Amazon.com, one cool dude; hipster king Michael Martens, who has never stopped helping and was always there when we needed him; and Count Smokula, the reigning proponent of Smokulism.

We owe a debt of gratitude to Richard Raynor of Raynor and Dove, who continues to provide sound legal advice. In many ways he is the Dr. Gonzo to our collective Hunter S. Thompson.

A very special thanks and neverending love to Samantha Sackin for her understanding, willingness to tell us when we were wrong (pulling no punches, by the way), and going above and beyond the call of duty for all things UglyTown.

And where would we be without our families? Our deepest debt goes to Jim Pascoe, Patty Pascoe, Jason Pascoe, Catherine Lehnertz, Ronald Fassbender, Mark Fassbender, Linda Soltis, and Carla Fassbender for their continued love and encouragement.

During the course of writing *By the Balls*, we were lucky enough to have met illustrator Salvatore Murdocca. His life philosophy, already dangerously close to our own, has been an ongoing source of inspiration.

Profound appreciation to Jackie Estrada, Chad Hermann, and Liesel Schulz, for their hours of editing and polishing. Of course, thanks to artist Paul Pope and logo designer "Dandy" Don Simpson (check out his weekly serial at http://fiasco.telerama.com) for their splendid work and friendship.

Finally, in what could pass for product endorsements, LaVazza Gold and Ketel One provided us with the occasional (slightly) sinful refreshment.

—TMF & JPP
July, 1998

ABOUT THE AUTHORS

DASHIELL LOVELESS

Dashiell Loveless is a journalist for the Testacy City *Herald-Tribune*, where his exposés on Testacy City's criminal element have garnered numerous awards. He is also the author of numerous short stories, including the cult favorite, "Raspberry Jack." *By the Balls* is his first novel.

Although he lives and works in Testacy City, he has disappeared with the advent of his research into the events surrounding the enigmatic murder of the Red Hat. He prefers to drink Bass Ale. His blood type is O positive.